For Max and Nunina

My sincere thanks go out to M. R. Tapia for his expertise and hard work in helping me make this book what it is today. Thanks, brother, it is very much appreciated!

an ARMY of SKIN

MORGAN K. TANNER

ONE

I wiped the corpse's sticky blood and my own sweat from my brow. Taking a step back I cast a critical eye over the finished piece. Not bad for a first attempt, but in reality it was nowhere near the picture in the textbook.

I took a deep, calming breath and scratched at my tired eyes. But when they reopened the structure seemed even more amateurish than seconds earlier. The limbs, dissected into eight pieces, were arranged like a grotesque Jenga construct. The torso was the foundation of the piece while the head sat proudly on top like a putrefying sentry. As I stared, one of the forearms slid outwards, the slimy surface acting as a lubricant. The whole structure collapsed with a wet *schlopp* sound.

"Bitch," I screamed, before marching forward and kicking the head against the wall. The pain erupted through my toe as the bloody cranium rattled against the brickwork. I hopped for a second or so, wiggling my leg, as if that would do anything against the throbbing that was taking hold in my foot. I lashed out at the dismembered body parts that now lay in a slick pool of blackened blood covering most of the floor. My standing foot gave way and I slipped. Instinctively my hand shot out to cushion the fall. The raw muscle of one of the legs was wet and tacky against my skin. I looked at my now glove-less hand and cursed myself for removing them so soon.

"Idiot," I sighed.

My attempts to stand wouldn't have been out of place in a slapstick comedy movie, but I was far from a jovial mood. When I made it back to my feet I clenched my fists and scowled at the pieces, as if that would somehow shame them into rearranging themselves back into the neat pile I'd spent hours working on. The head was grinning at me from the opposite corner of the room. The teeth bright white against the shiny, red muscles like a zipper stitched on to a juicy tomato.

I composed myself with some breathing exercises Dr Mellick had once shown me. It was a good technique. You breathe in deeply, push out your chest, and think about something from your childhood; an interesting textbook, a favourite toy, or a trip to the seaside. Then you exhale smoothly as though you are blowing through a straw. It was a mild form of self-hypnosis and always worked like a charm. Thankfully this was another of those occasions.

After a few moments I left the display to try and get my head together. I turned to the table behind me.

Although my attempt at post-mortal architecture had failed, not *miserably* but something fast approaching that, my other exploit this evening had faired rather better. Like an expensive wedding dress, her skin lay crease-free and undisturbed on the table in the corner of this cold, white room. The painted brickwork did give the suggestion of a mental institution, which was rather ironic. How could someone who was labelled insane make something as marvellous as this? Well?

Exactly.

I picked up the dress of skin and held it aloft, as though I were about to hang it out to dry. I was careful not to finger it too forcibly, although I wasn't sure if this was entirely necessary. This being my first attempt at flaying a human I could remember, naturally I was unaware of how the skin would react to being fondled in this way.

Funny, though, I had little memory of the actual killing

and dismembering of this woman. It was a little annoying, to tell you the truth. Perhaps it was the excitement of my first time, like losing your virginity. You spend years picturing it then, when the time finally comes, it's over in seconds and you ask yourself whether you actually just imagined the whole thing. I made a mental note to savour the next one.

I placed the skin, now slightly crinkled, back on the table and consulted the textbook. The pages of the tome were well worn and many of them ripped, but the pictures and instructions were as clear as day. I was only on page 3, and a brief flick through the book made me consider giving up right there and then. There were over 400 pages in the damn thing. Although I wasn't going to beat myself up if I couldn't finish it all. Maybe I'd skip a few that looked too hard.

In fact, on page 213 there was a particularly difficult-looking piece. The subject, which was what all the victims were referred to in there, was suspended by its hair, with its elbows and knees hyperextended, the fingers and toes gnarled. It had the appearance of a floating spider-person. Maybe I'd give that one a miss. Like I said, I didn't have to do every single one. It's the taking part that matters, right?

I put the book down and stared at the face on the table. I removed the bottle of pills from my pocket with a shaky hand and swallowed two. I didn't know what they were but they were prescribed by Dr Mellick and made me feel better at times like this. It wasn't that important to give them a name.

The face almost seemed to look up at me from the table. "Not bad, not bad at all," I muttered, "but I'll do better next time."

"Yes, you will," answered a voice.

I spun around as panic and fear began battling for supremacy in my head and chest. "Who the fuck said that?" I screamed at the empty room, my echoing voice the only response. The sweat dripped from my quivering face. The salty discharge stung my eyes but I was too gripped with terror to clear them. It must have been minutes that I stood there, too scared to move or say anything. Was someone else here?

The breathing exercises did their job again. I finally began to believe my eyes and convinced myself that my ears were just fucking with me. It wouldn't have been the first time. It was OK, I was definitely alone.

My eyes returned to the skin. Had it shifted its position?

I froze. My mouth hung open and my throat clenched. "What?" I finally asked it. But the skin lay lifeless and silent.

TWO

A thousand phones rang without pause as an army of sick people battled through the front entrance. Like the true hero I was, I cowered in the kitchen behind the reception area. I hoped my colleagues would deal with this shit while I made myself a coffee. A strong, sugary punch of caffeine was exactly what I needed this morning.

I hadn't slept much after the previous night's hard work and now I felt both mentally and physically shattered. Murdering and skinning is something you need to rest after, and I really hadn't. A bit like losing your virginity. I really must stop comparing killing to sex, you're probably beginning to get the wrong impression of me.

I closed my eyes and leaned against the wall for a micro-sleep while the kettle boiled. It was done in seconds. As the roaring sound of the water faded to nothing, those bastard phones took the baton and pummelled my ears with their unrelenting, incessant ringing. The shrill emanated from inside my head, and layers upon layers of that same irritating note only heightened my annoyance.

My hand shook as I spooned the coffee into the mug. The pills hadn't started working yet. I rubbed my forehead with my fingertips, attempting to nurse the fast-approaching headache.

"Mr King," shrieked a voice from behind me, "you're needed on the desk. Get your drink and get to work, understand?" Veronica's sarcastic use of 'Mr King' never failed to irk me, and she knew it.

I stirred my coffee and said nothing in response.

"*Trevor.*" Her voice was like nails on, not a chalkboard, but the inside of my own skull. She could see I wasn't feeling well this morning but sympathy wasn't a word she was familiar with. Why did bosses have to be such ball-busters?

"Yeah, I'm coming," I said. I glanced at her through half-open lids, observing the hands on her hips and scowl on her face. I often wondered if she continuously sucked on sour sweets, as her face appeared like she did. Her body shape certainly suggested this was the case.

Her eyes bored into the back of my head from below her sharp eyebrows as I entered the reception area and sat down at my desk.

"Heavy night out with the lads was it?" said a woman, Jill I think her name was, from along the desk.

"Yeah, something like that." I wish. I couldn't remember the last time I'd socialised with anyone.

An old man stood before me and opened his mouth to say something. I held my hand up to shush him as I picked up the still-ringing phone. The man frowned and muttered something under his breath.

"Hello, Millennium Surgery, Trevor speaking, how can I help you?" I was on autopilot. The voice at the other end stammered, surprised he'd got an answer. He prattled on about some sickness bug or something, not letting me get a word in. This was how the calls usually went. "So you want an appointment?" I interrupted. He did.

The morning continued in much the same, monotonous fashion. People were either ranting to me on the phone, or moaning at me in person from the other side of the desk. Being a doctor's receptionist was never my dream in life. I admit I was an odd addition to the team, a guy in his twenties isn't usually seen in this type of work environment. But I'd been given this job out of pity. With everything I'd been through recently it was time to get myself back to supposed normality.

By 11 o'clock the morning rush had eased somewhat allowing me to stretch back and try to relax. A bald dude with an attitude stormed over to me. I slowly leaned forward, doing my best to force an approachable smile onto my face.

"I've been waiting for a doctor to come out and see my dad for three days now." No 'hello' obviously. "This is ridiculous, what you gonna do about it, son?"

Son?

"And what's your father's name, sir?" I clicked the mouse to try and make it look like I was with it.

"Really?" he huffed. "Do I have to go through all this again?"

I don't need to go into the specifics here. Frankly, it would bore you to tears. But the conversation ended with me taking his details and passing on another message to the doctor timetabled for call-outs that day. Although I'd gone to a certain degree of effort on his dad's behalf, I got no word of thanks from the bald attitude. But I've come to expect this by now.

All the time he was complaining to me I couldn't help picturing him as that spider-person on page 213 of my textbook, my instruction manual.

I stood over the toaster and watched my bread blossom from white to gold to black. As I stared into the hot chasm of metal I thought about my plan, my vengeance.

"No sandwiches today? You're going to set off the fire alarm, you know." I jumped, my daydream suddenly interrupted. Dr Mellick entered the staff room and flicked on the kettle, a wry smile crossing his lips. "How burnt did you want your toast exactly?" He'd always taken an interest in my eating habits at work, asking what was in my sandwiches, where I bought my snacks, things like that. It was a bit weird really, but maybe he was genuinely interested in what I was eating. My lunch was always pretty healthy so perhaps he was just innocently making sure that I was eating properly. Still, it was weird.

I watched him as he spooned the coffee into his mug with a meticulous swagger. His black, bushy eyebrows were raised as always, as though he was constantly awaiting the reply to a question. His dark, thick-rimmed glasses did nothing to lighten his appearance, what with his two-day old stubble and dark, crater-like wrinkles on his forehead. He was a hairy man, probably the only thing we actually shared in common.

His deep, brown eyes glanced up at me and I suddenly realised that I was sneering at him. I quickly replaced it with a smile. "I like it black, it's the only way to enjoy your food. Desecrated beyond recognition. Like a burn victim, you know."

He smiled at my exuberance. I'd no qualms about sharing my passion for horror and the macabre, and he knew it, *admired* it even.

"I imagine that it's a human in there, burning to death, knowing who their killer is and what he'll do with them once they're dead and gone." I laughed as though I'd just delivered him a classic one-liner.

"You are one on your own, you know that?" Dr Mellick frowned with a head tilt, as though he was analysing me. OK, he was my GP, but he was also a colleague, and this was definitely a colleague moment. Although, can doctors ever switch off?

He took his coffee and sat in one of the staff rooms comfy armchairs. He placed the mug on the table next to him and picked up his broadsheet, rustling it in that way pretentious people do.

My toast popped up like a gunshot. I ignored it and stared at Dr Mellick. Only his hands and crossed legs were visible behind his giant newspaper. My hands balled into fists and the tension shot up my arms. I felt my pulse quicken and sweat form on my brow.

He just sat there, oblivious to my rage.

You see, I had unfinished business with Dr James Mellick. He was the one who cut a couple of corners to land me this job months ago and to him it was probably me who owed him. But he would be the one to pay. He probably didn't even remember my mom.

I loved her more than anything, something he could probably never even begin to imagine. I don't care what anyone else would say, our bond was so special and, I thought, unbreakable.

Well, she's dead now and it's all his fault.

For weeks she'd been suffering with headaches and on-ly after she'd passed out in the supermarket did she finally bother the good doctor with her pain. He'd basically laughed her out of the room. Paracetamol and a sleep were his recommendations.

She'd been too terrified to go back, preferring instead to lie awake every night with the intense throbbing attack-ing her brain. It was awful to see her in that state, beyond words. I'd tried to get her help. I'd called the surgery nu-merous times requesting, no, *demanding* her to be seen. But on the two occasions someone had visited, she'd refused to see them and screamed at them to be left alone. It was-n't even Dr Mellick who'd attended, he was probably too busy on a seminar or flirting with the reception staff and nurses. I didn't think this at the time, though. It was only after working with him that I saw the real Dr Mellick. Dr Heartless Bastard more like.

I begged her to allow him to see her but she was so stubborn. "Please, not him, I don't want *him* in this house. You understand me, Trevor?" she'd wailed. If she wasn't as weak as she had been we would have argued, but I couldn't put her through that. She was so terrified that he'd call her a hypochondriac again. The prospect of being la-belled 'mentally unstable' was what frightened Mom more than anything. None of my desperate pleas would ever change her mind.

It all happened so fast. One evening she cried herself to sleep as I cried in the next room, the next morning she never woke up. A brain tumour was what killed her, pretty massive it was by the end. Not a *migraine*, as Dr Mellick had originally diagnosed, and simple Paracetamol and rest had not cured her.

But did he care? Possibly he felt a little put out at having to fill in extra paperwork regarding her death, but I'm sure that was all. There was no apology and he never even had the decency to return my calls. He'd washed his hands of her and I could never forgive him for that.

Mom was everything to me, the only one who ever understood me. And now all I want is to take everything from that bastard. I hadn't taken this job with the idea of concocting this whole vengeance scheme. In fact I felt like I could give something back, make sure that others wouldn't have to go through the same ordeal that me and Mom had suffered. I'm no doctor and have little knowledge about anything medical. But I understand when people are sick and need treatment, only for these so-called 'experts' to decide they aren't worth the hassle.

Seeing his arrogant swagger, his blatant disregard for taking patients seriously, his 'I'm the most important man in this building' attitude; it brewed the hatred in me like an insidious, noxious cocktail. He derided patients' symptoms and complaints to colleagues, planned golfing weekends mere moments after delivering terminal test results. He did all this assuming that no reception staff, such as myself, were listening. Oh, but I *was* listening, *Doctor*.

I munched on my toast, still staring at the man and his paper as my head cleared. I spoke before my brain had a chance to stop me. "So I checked out that book, you know, the one about the skin." I frowned in confusion, why the hell was I bringing that up? Dr Mellick had lent it to me a few months ago, said I might find it interesting.

I'm sure he'd forgotten even giving it to me, he never asked if I'd read it. I could have kicked myself for mentioning it. I certainly wasn't planning on doing so, not now, not to him.

He flicked his paper down and looked at me with his black caterpillar eyebrows raised in anticipation. "Really? And what did you think?"

"Yeah, it's – err, pretty fucked up." I fumbled some more charred toast into my mouth to hide my mumbling.

"Well that depends on how you look at it. I believe that it is anything but. The human body is a wondrous creation. To marvel at the complexity of it and appreciate the workings of the various systems, you can almost understand why some people believe it was designed by some higher being. But when you see the size of the medical textbooks that detail what can go *wrong* with it, it's obvious we're a very flawed design."

I continued to stand and eat, looking down on him made me feel a little less inferior than he was trying to make me. Doctors have a tendency to do that; patronise you, even the nice ones.

"The guy that wrote that book is a genius. All the bodies in there were willing volunteers, donating themselves to him and his work. Many of them are from medical backgrounds themselves." He'd put his paper in his lap now, his eyes fixated on me as he spoke. He was on to one of his favourite topics and it would be difficult to escape him for the moment. I smiled, though, he was simply fuelling the fire.

He was still talking but I'd lost track. My tired eyes rolled in their sockets and for the briefest of moments I pictured Dr Mellick as a talking skin, laid out on the table of my kill room. No, that wasn't the plan, he was to suffer much more agony than that.

"I've already filled in my application," he said, "you might be seeing me in a future edition one day." Was that a joke? He wasn't smiling but that didn't mean anything.

"You don't mind people seeing your dead cock then?" His stony-faced reaction to my attempted humour proved he hadn't been joking.

"What would I care? I'd be dead," he frowned, as though I'd offended him somehow.

He pulled up his paper with an air of finality. I finished my toast and dropped the plate into the sink before heading out of the door.

"Besides," Dr Mellick shouted after me, "I'm hung like a shire horse." I didn't answer, my temples throbbed as the regular lunchtime headache entered the building right on cue.

Come to think of it, I really *could* picture him in that textbook.

The lockup wasn't too far from my house, a ten minute walk or so, but I always took the car. I'm lazy like that. I'd headed home first for a shower and, having washed away the remnants of the working day, returned to my kill room.

THREE

The place actually belonged to Dr Mellick. I know, right? I'd been renting it from him for the last few weeks. I say renting, but I didn't pay him anything. I'd told him my band needed somewhere to practice, somewhere quiet so we could make a lot of noise without disturbing anyone. Not that I'm in a band, or play an instrument, or even know anyone who does.

I think Dr Mellick had hoped he'd been a rock star instead of a GP, though. Why else would he rent this place to me for free? He'd mentioned, in passing, that he owned this lockup but never used it and was thinking of cancelling the lease. That's when I'd bustled into the conversation, spinning some yarn about my failing music career. Strangely he'd encouraged me to move my band in, said that he'd like to help.

Little did he know he was actually aiding me in his own downfall. I'd been on the lookout for a space, and the good doctor had been only too accommodating in providing me with one.

The place would have been perfect for a metal band, though. Especially now it had witnessed its first murder.

I rolled up the metal shutters and the stench of rotting flesh invaded my nostrils like a necrotic cancer, slapping me in the face like a putrid, wet fish. I recoiled and retched. It was bad, sickeningly bad. I suppose I shouldn't have been surprised, though, there *was* a dead body in there, skinned and all.

Before leaving last night I had attempted to tidy up a little. I'd piled the pieces of the body in the corner, not in the least bit aptly, and left the skin neatly curing on the table.

I picked up the textbook and opened a page at random. Another skinning, but this time the remaining body had been arranged in a heart shape. The head, legs, arms, feet, hands, and the torso, all removed and laid out in the shape of love, coloured in scarlet. Perhaps the picture had red paint, come to think of it, but real blood would look much cooler. Plus there was still plenty on the floor after last night's. Although it was already blackening and had lumps of slimy clot scattered through it.

Hopefully my attempt tonight would be more akin to the instructions.

I put the leftovers of my previous night's work carefully into a black bag, as though I were cleaning up the remnants of a particularly mental party. If I got into work early enough the next day I could borrow the key to the dumpster where they put the contaminated waste. It would be incinerated that same day so, providing no one saw me, I'd be out of trouble. Perhaps a bit risky, but never mind.

I left the shutters open slightly to try and let a draft in. It wasn't ideal but without an air freshener with me it was the best I could manage. It wasn't like the industrial estate where the lockup was located was teeming with people.

It was getting dark outside and although the place was still far off being clean, it was time. Time to find another victim. But where, and who?

Prostitutes. I know, I know, it's so cliché, but it's no co-incidence sadistic people prey upon them. My tip is to seek out the ones that look young and a little terrified, the inexperienced ones, if you will. Those who look like they've been on the game for a long time tend to put up more of a fight, I'm sure. I say all this like I'm some kind of expert, but I'm not. It just seems like common sense to me. Last night's fitted into the 'young and naïve' category, and she was no trouble. I think. The details remain a little hazy.

I sound like some kind of monster, but that couldn't be farther from the truth. Remember, I'm doing all of this for a purpose. An act of vengeance. This is all leading to something great.

I'd like to think that I don't really have the look of someone who would have to pay for sex. I'm young, not fat, and don't have a face that looks like I've been beaten with a shovel then pissed on with acidic alien blood. I dress kind of cool, too, even if I do say so myself. Nothing too fashionable, nothing too outdated. I suppose I'm *almost-retro-chic*, that's not a thing but it may be one day. You heard it here first.

I'd thought, or rather hoped, that the hookers would look at me strangely, telling me that I shouldn't be here, that if they weren't on the game then they would sure like to hook up with me for some 'real' sexy time. But alas, I was wrong. As soon as I 'hit the stretch' I was, there's no other word for it, accosted.

"Hey there, handsome, wanna party?"

"I bet you got a big hard dick for me."

"I can't wait to suck you dry, big boy."

And there was me thinking that all the corny lines in the movies were made up. No, it seems like that is exactly how these ladies speak to their would-be clients. And there I was, the same as all those losers with bald heads and big, greasy beer-bellies in their stained long coats and failing marriages, desperate to find someone to stick it into.

The realisation that they saw me as just a regular punter both saddened and irritated me. But there was no time to dwell on this, I needed to get my head together and my game-face on. There was work to do.

I waved away the advances of the whores as they approached me like a horde of the undead in the grimy night air. If need be I could probably outrun them, what with their chicken legs and giant heels. They didn't seem like they were ready for running.

Then I saw her, in front of a boarded up shop with peeling paint and graffiti; *the one*. She was trying to hide herself in the shadows but the cherry from her cigarette held between quivering fingers gave away her position. I cleared my throat and walked towards her with almost a swagger. As she noticed me approaching she slid herself further inside the doorway, but then realised the move was pointless.

"Hello there," I greeted her, looking around to try and act like I was nervous. I even told her, "Sorry, I'm a little nervous. This is my first time doing – this."

You could tell that whoever had coached her had said to keep a hard-looking expression, but it was obvious this wasn't really her. Her story was probably tragic. She could have only been nineteen, and perhaps that was being generous. She took a long drag on her cigarette and blew the smoke into my face. I held my breath at the sickening smell, never once taking my eyes from her frankly frightened body. She wore a black mini skirt with fishnets and a sparkling red top, displaying a tiny cleavage.

"You got money?" her voice wavered from bright red lips on a face that was just skin, bones, and foundation. She really could have done with a good meal.

"Yeah, I'm not sure how much you charge, though. I mean what kinds of things do you –"

"Let's see it then," she cut me off. I glanced around, making sure her pimp wasn't hiding somewhere waiting to rob me, then pulled out my wad of cash.

Her eyes widened at the sight. For such a young girl she had quite pronounced wrinkles on her forehead.

"Is this going to be enough?"

Her face told me that it definitely was. "You got somewhere we can go?"

"Sure, my car's just around the corner, we can drive to my place if that's cool. Is that what usually happens?"

"Yeah, usually," she said to herself. Her gaze was still drawn to her fee, crumpled in my hand. I handed it all over so she'd know I wasn't some sort of time waster.

We didn't speak during the short walk to my battered old BMW. It was a rusted piece of shit, but it was *my* rusted piece of shit. I swallowed a couple of pills, hoping that they'd calm me down somewhat, but she didn't notice. Her eyes were anywhere but on me.

Once inside the car I made sure she fastened her seatbelt (safety first!) and started the engine without locking the doors. I wanted her to feel safe and not start attacking me or something. There would be plenty of time for the realisation of her desperate situation to fully sink in.

"So, you got a name?" I phrased the question nonchalantly, trying to sound cool, even though I'd just picked up a prostitute.

"Alectra." She sounded bored.

"Electra?" I coughed a small chuckle.

"No, *A*lectra, with an A. Do you mind if I smoke?"

The suggestion disgusted me. "Not at all." I opened the window for her as she lit up. "Alectra, hey? That's an interesting name, it's pretty. It suits you, you know?"

"It's not my real name," she huffed. Yeah, I'd sort of guessed that already but I was trying to be charming.

"You wanna know mine?"

"Not really."

"Well, it's James. James Mellick." I glanced at her when she didn't respond. She stared out of the window, puffing on her cigarette. I wasn't sure if she hadn't heard me with the wind blowing into the car, or whether she was just ignoring me. OK, it was probably the latter.

I left it there. There seemed little point in trying to continue the conversation. If I really was planning on having sex with her I may have been a little annoyed. But seeing as though I was driving her to her death, I couldn't be that pissed off she was giving me the cold shoulder. In truth she was probably scared shitless of me.

She had every right to be.

A few minutes later the street lights faded as we turned into the industrial estate where the factories were either shut for the night or, as most were, closed down for good. Alectra shifted in her seat at the sight of the darkened abandoned buildings.

"Here we are then, honey,"

"This is your place?" she said, frowning at the building.

"Well no, it's not my house but we can't go there tonight." *I can't murder you there.*

I got out of the car and opened her door, offering my hand. She refused it. Alectra stared wide-eyed at the lock-up's dirty metal shutters and sneered.

"Don't worry, it's much cosier inside. I'll drive you back afterwards," I said. "It shouldn't take long, it doesn't usually." My attempted humour was doing little to reassure her everything would be OK.

As the shutters rolled up the stink of decaying offal collided violently with my nostrils. I hoped that her sense of smell had been depleted by the years of cigarettes and nose powder. It must have been, as she wandered inside without a hint of argument.

"So, can I get you a drink?" I closed the shutters quickly with a brief glance outside to check we were unseen.

"No."

"Not thirsty, eh? That's OK, though I don't think there's much in anyway."

I'd semi-planned how this was going to go but now we were here I was a little lost. I left her to survey the dirty room while I walked to the other side of the partitioning wall to check my tools. With each step my boots peeled away yet more of the sticky residue from last night's work.

I'd felt apprehensive during the journey here, despite the confidence I displayed in the car. Now inside, nerves tingled, pulses pounded, and my palms were slick yet cold. I wondered whether I'd actually be able to do it.

Were the pills ever going to start working? Maybe they

were already, I couldn't tell. My anxiousness was all I was aware of. If only I could have remembered how I'd done it last night, that would have made me feel better. I turned to the table where I'd left the skin, hoping that seeing it would snap me out of this apprehension and calm my nerves; a motivational tool to show me the way.

In that moment everything slowed down, except my pulse. It was hammering at my neck like a tiny drummer was practicing in there. The sweat was pouring from me. I stood, frozen on the spot in abject panic.

The skin was missing. The skin was fucking missing.

"Fuck," I yelled, louder than I intended to.

Alectra shouted from the other side of the wall. "OK then, let's do it." Maybe she thought it was an instruction.

I couldn't find the words to reply. My eyes darted in their sockets, desperately searching for my prized asset. I looked under the table, already knowing that it wasn't there but having to check all the same. I stood up straight and scratched at my head, wincing as my nails drew blood. "What the fuck?"

Had someone been here? No, there was no sign of a break in, the shutters were just as I'd left them. There was no one else who had a key for this place, except...

"No, no way, he can't have." My thoughts were transferred into words. "No, no, no, *no*." Why would Dr Mellick have come here? He'd no reason to. To him it was an abandoned old space that he no longer had use for. He hadn't visited in months, not since I'd been using it. Had he?

I had no time to think further. The scream that came from the other side of the wall was like nothing I'd ever heard before. She'd probably screamed last night, too. The sweat was unabating, pooling under my armpits and in my ass crack. I turned my head and walked instinctively, yet hesitantly, towards the terrible sound.

Alectra's screams were desperate. They were muffled, as though she was being gagged. Whatever was going on, she was putting up a fight.

My heart doubled in size and work-rate. I couldn't tell whether my fear was for someone else completing the job I'd come here to do, or whether I was scared that I was next. Whatever it was, I couldn't just stand here and do nothing.

I pushed out my chest and reared up like a wild animal about to confront a hungry predator. But as I rounded the wall and saw Alectra on her knees, and not in the way that most prostitutes kneel, the terror really set in.

Shadows surrounded her. The black shapes seemed to dance on her skin as her body contorted like she was bound. Her cries had disappeared and the only sound was my own retching. Her head flew towards the concrete with a wet snap. Her nose connected with the grimy concrete floor, blood spattering around her head. She slumped forward as her body relaxed and lay there, twitching for a second or two.

My belly gurgled and my throat clenched before the vomit erupted. The room began to spin.

I could feel consciousness rapidly deserting me. As I slumped forward I saw the shadows return. A ghostly shape slithered past me, and the draft cooled the sweat on my brow. My mind tried to deny what my eyes had seen but as I blacked out I knew this was no illusion.

It was the missing skin from the table. It was alive.

FOUR

I had no idea how long I'd been out. Silence surrounded me. Although there were no windows in the lockup I knew it was still dark outside. I wondered whether I'd been in a fight. The bruises erupted in my muscles and under my skin like branding irons. My joints creaked as though they were ready to fall apart.

It took a few moments for me to stand and when I got there I had to hold on to the wall to keep my balance. I felt drunk. Swaying, I scrunched my eyes then opened them, hoping this had all been a terrible nightmare.

I stared up at Alectra's body. She was suspended upside down with wires around her feet, and her legs spread like a pornographic, inverted Jesus. From her sliced-open stomach spewed intestines that bound her arms to her torso and wrapped around her neck like a slimy, hungry serpent. A pool of blood and visceral juice collected and spread beneath her. Her muscles glowed like a neon afterbirth. Although skinless, her face still displayed evidence of a horrific death.

The spectacle both disgusted and excited me. It was a damn fine job. I recognised the display, of course, it was exactly like the picture on the next page of the textbook. It should have been the one I accomplished tonight, although the work that had gone into her was much more exquisitely done than I ever could have managed.

21

I had to get my shit together. Who had done this? In my mind I saw the skin from last night's, my first foray into this macabre pastime, flowing past me. No, that was impossible. Perhaps it was my recent bloodlust playing tricks on me. I shook my head with contorted neck muscles, trying to rid these ridiculous thoughts.

"I told you you would do better, and you have. Are you not proud of your work?" The cold voice startled me and I fell to my knees, it felt safer down there. Against the wishes of my contracted muscles, I turned my head to the source of the voice behind me. I saw what I feared I would.

The skin floated in the corner of the room. Even without eyes the thing stared at me and I got a strange feeling of warmth inside. I'd always assumed that facial expressions were comprised of muscles and features, as well as the eyes. But this thing, this mere flap of skin, gave me a proud look that I comprehended fully.

"Well, what do you think?" it asked me, without a throat, without vocal chords, without a goddamn *tongue*.

I stood, somehow it felt more appropriate to be standing when I addressed this thing, even though my body screamed at me in defiance. "What the fuck are you— *talking* about?" I glanced around the room, I even pinched myself, as crazy as that sounds, but I didn't wake up.

"Trevor, have you forgotten what you did last night?" The skin wheezed like a smoker but its mouth didn't move. It looked like a character in a badly dubbed horror movie. "You are getting better at this."

I coughed and spat the residue on to the floor in front of the hideous shroud of leather.

"Your plan is coming together. Look." Something small glistened in the centre of the room. I frowned and trudged over to it, my legs refusing to work properly. When I reached the object I crouched, then let out a stifled cry. A metal fountain pen gleamed at me, the italic letters on the side were ones I knew all too well. *Dr James Mellick.*

I reached for it.

"Do not touch it. It needs to stay there, right there."

I stood, a little easier this time. "So he *was* here?" My thoughts were beginning to assemble themselves but the skin just stared at me with a cold vacancy. "*He* killed her? But I thought..."

"No, he was never here, but one would assume he was."

I took a deep breath. Maybe I was going crazy, maybe I had done the elaborate art piece with Alectra's body after I'd brutally murdered her. Maybe this living piece of dead tissue in front of me was all in my head, my way of severing myself from the horrors I'd committed, and the many more that I would need to do to complete my work.

With shaking fingers I took out the bottle of pills from my pocket. Shit, how I needed one, or ten. I fumbled one into my mouth and closed my eyes, willing the medicine to flow through my body and cleanse my confused brain.

All of a sudden my muscles stopped twitching, my deep aching subsided, and my mind became lucid. I opened my eyes and looked directly into the empty, black caverns where eyes should have been in the remnants of my first kill, the one that now floated before me.

"Yes, my plan is going exactly to, err, plan," I told the skin. "I am ready to continue."

"Patience, Trevor. You must go now. We shall take care of this."

My eyebrows furrowed. "*We?*"

"Yes," spoke another voice. If I had to describe it I would say it was similar to the skin's only *fresher*. As if from nowhere, Alectra's skin floated alongside that of my first victim. They could have been sisters.

"Do not worry about a thing. Now go."

I had not a coherent thought in my mind. Was it the pills? It *had* to be the pills. But it all seemed so real. I mumbled something, I'm not sure what it was, but I obeyed the skin's words and opened the shutters before stumbling outside into the crisp, night air.

It was like my brain had shut itself off from believing what I'd just seen. It had one goal in mind; to get me out of here and back home where I could get some much needed sleep. But would anything ever be the same again?

FIVE

I arrived home at around 6 in the morning. I'd no idea how it had taken me so long to get there. Since leaving the lockup my memory was a blur. I was completely shattered but right now sleep was the last thing on my mind.

Just what I had I been up to for the last few hours?

An ice cold shower did nothing to drag me back to normality. Although clean I could still smell the rotten, coppery stench of the skins all around me as I dried myself. My body ached and my eyes looked like I had thick eyeshadow applied. But apart from looking like I'd been out drinking all night, I was strangely satisfied with my appearance. Nothing a smart tie and an ironed shirt wouldn't fix.

My shirt was creased and the iron wouldn't work. Oh, and my best tie was missing, somehow. Too knackered to even attempt to look for it I left for work, chucking back a couple of pills as I closed the front door. So what if I looked like abject hangover? At least I'd make it to work on time.

"Everything OK, Trevor?" asked one of my colleagues behind the desk as I made my way stealthily to my seat. I couldn't remember her name. I mean, I *knew* her, but this morning my mind was elsewhere, obviously. All I was aware of was the screen in front of me.

There was a red '!' flashing at the bottom of the monitor. This meant an important message needed to be read. With a groan I clicked on it.

The memo was a paragraph or two long, and I made little sense of it. But I got the gist; Dr Mellick was sick. Illness happened occasionally and when it did it was a complete ball ache for us receptionites. It meant phoning patients to cancel appointments and, where possible, re-arranging the times to fit in as many as we could with the other doctors.

Thank fuck I'd chuffed a couple of pills before leaving home. I'd been shouted at, called all sorts of names, and been physically threatened. These people seemed to think it was *my* fault the doctor was sick.

"Listen, you," came a voice. I rolled my eyes with closed lids to disguise my disgust. "You people have can-celled my appointment this morning, it ain't on. I need to see the doctor, I'm sick. Excuse me, are you even listening to me?"

I took a deep breath to prepare myself for another ar-gument, and slowly opened my eyes.

I shrieked. It wasn't a very manly thing to do I'll admit, but the horrific image came so unexpectedly my body and mind weren't ready for it. Before me stood a rotten old man, his face wrinkled and leathery. But the man was just skin. He floated in front of me without eyes, only empty sockets that looked like twin entrances to some kind of demonic abyss.

I thrust myself from the desk and as I jumped to my feet my ankle caught the leg of the chair. I fell, crashing to the floor in a pathetic crumpled mess. I clawed at the car-pet to try and correct myself, but I struggled. I must have looked like Gregor Samsa there, desperately trying to stand as if on a frozen lake. There were people around me, ask-ing me if I was OK and offering me their hands. I looked up to find yet more skins surrounding me, their absent expressions communicating such horrific intentions. I pulled my arm back and screamed some more.

"Leave me the fuck alone," I yelled, finally making it to my feet. I backed out of the reception area as the monsters remained still, staring at me like I was a strange exhibit. "Fuck off." I retreated from the grotesque forms then smashed the back of my head on a shelf which had always been there. I stumbled forward and fell to my knees.

"Trevor? Trevor what's wrong?" On all fours I raised my head. Around me were the concerned faces of my colleagues. I'd caused quite a scene. There were patients huddled around the desk hoping to catch a glimpse at the psycho freaking out.

"I'm... I'm fine." I snatched my hand away as one of them tried to help me up. I winced at the exertion but once standing I sneered at the onlooking patients. "Enjoying the show, you sickos?" which was quite apt really, seeing as they *were* waiting to see a doctor.

Veronica stomped in and for the first time ever she actually looked worried. "Come on, upstairs," she said, as though I was some sort of kid, "let's get you a drink."

I blew out some air, relieved she wasn't angry with me. But that was short lived.

She followed me up and when we were out of earshot of the patients said, "You're a disgrace, you look like shit. Clean yourself up."

I was on the verge of tears. "Please, Veronica, I don't feel too good. I need to get some rest, this won't happen again I promise."

My pleas fell on deaf ears.

"Five minutes, no longer. Sort yourself and get back to work. There's no way you're going home. Self-inflicted illness is not an excuse for time off. Maybe the next time you're out drinking till all hours you will consider your work responsibilities." She stormed off without a second glance at me.

I sat in the empty staff room with a hot coffee cupped in my shaking hands. For the first time since this all started I questioned my sanity. Was I losing it? Seeing people as floating skins was definitely not normal, but come to think of it neither was talking to them.

I wiggled my toes and stretched out my legs, it brought a satisfying ache to my muscles and seemed to clear my mind a little. The pills would help, they usually did. I took a couple and relaxed back in the chair, waiting for the magic to engulf me.

It was half an hour before I felt confident enough to brave downstairs. Veronica didn't come looking for me which was a small mercy. As I walked behind reception I felt like a stranger in a Western saloon, such was the hush that descended around me. I ignored the gazes and sat in my usual place.

"Hey there, Trevor, how you doing?" Anna, *that* was her name. Now I'd had my mini-breakdown I remembered.

"Yeah, you know." That would have to do.

She gave me a comforting hand on the shoulder. "Look, we're OK back here for the time being, but we need Dr Mellick's patient files sorted. Do you want to go and do them, keep yourself out of the firing line for a bit?"

I could have hugged her. Although I felt a little better, the thought of having to converse with anyone would have surely brought my insanity straight back. Sorting out paperwork in a private room sounded like bliss.

"Anna," I said, "you're a darlin'." She smiled and nodded.

Dr Mellick's room was what you might have called organised chaos. I suppose that's doctors for you; they spend all their time being clever and self-righteous they never find the time to tidy up after themselves. He probably had a housekeeper at home to do all this kind of thing for him.

My head throbbed as I regarded the piles of papers and notes. His files were kept in the locked cabinet next to the desk but I needed some room to go through them. I stacked the papers up and made a bit of space on the old wooden desk.

The cabinet squealed as the metal runners passed over their rusty casters. In this day and age, where computers rule every moment of our lives, why we still relied on paper notes and filing cabinets, I'd never know. I had the list from reception and began to take out the appropriate files. For some reason the alphabet eluded me as I tried to make sense of the haphazardly arranged notes.

After far longer than it should have taken, I placed the required pile of notes on the desk. As I sat in front of them my mind began wandering about my plan. I stared into space, picturing the grotesque artwork constructed in Dr Mellick's lockup and the two skins that had promised me their help. Even though the skins I'd seen in reception had freaked me out, the ones I remembered from the lockup I still held fondly, weird as that sounds. Even though I was probably mad and yet to fully appreciate it, the thought that I had these two monsters on my side made the whole escapade a little more realistic.

And then it hit me. How it had taken so long I couldn't have said. Well, yes I could, I was hardly thinking straight today was I? Here I was in Dr Mellick's office, off sick for the day with no chance of him disturbing me, with all these personal possessions of his just waiting to be taken.

My plan, crude as it was, was to plant various bits of his stuff at the lockup. I was also planning to leave subtle clues on the streets where I picked up the prostitutes. If I was clever I could leave just enough evidence so that there was only one suspect in these gruesome murders. He would go down for this and I'd be there to watch it all unfold.

Was this all a bit extreme, though? Possibly, but he had to pay for what he did. And now here I was, like a kid in a sweet shop with bottomless pockets.

I turned Detective a little quicker than I would have thought, maybe I was in the wrong profession. I closed the rickety drawers and pulled open the bottom one of the cabinet. It was an effort, it seemed like the runners here weren't as well-oiled as the others. It was heavy, too, so I was intrigued to see what the good doctor was hiding in it.

There was a metal safe inside, locked, obviously. But if I knew doctors... Bullseye!

You see, doctors have lots of things locked up in their surgeries, so there are many keys that are needed. And because these doctors don't want the hassle of carrying these around with them everywhere, they usually hide them in their desk drawers. Well, Dr Mellick was no exception.

There was a keyring with 5 keys on it. The first one I tried was the right fit. I glanced around to make sure I was definitely alone, then opened the safe.

Inside was a notebook. It was pretty old judging by the cover; brown and stained with worn edges. I fingered through the pages. Most of the handwriting was illegible so I knew it was Dr Mellick's.

There were calculations for bills, addresses for garages and dry cleaners, lots of medical jargon and references to papers he'd read; but mostly it was just scribble.

I glanced up at the photographs on his desk. He was smiling with his wife and two daughters. I think they were about my age, perhaps a little older. Next to that was a picture of a tiny baby. I supposed *that* would be one way to get back at him. I rubbished the idea, even *I* wasn't that sick or heartless.

I scanned the pages in the notebook, paying little attention to what was written until my eyes fell upon something I recognised. *St Luke's Hospital*, he'd scribbled. Why did I recognise the name of that place? It wasn't somewhere in use anymore, I was pretty sure of that. There'd been no admissions made to a place of that name, and believe me I had to write up many letters for hospital admissions in my job. No, it was something else.

I planted my elbows on the desk, remembering my hangover-like state, and rubbed my fingers on my temples. "St Luke's, St Luke's," I mumbled in deep thought. I regretted taking the mind-numbing pills, I really needed all thought-centres on max right now. Mom had spoken of that place. Suddenly the memory forced its way into my mind.

"No, Trevor I'm not going to see him again, he'll just send me off to that horrid hospital. That's where they send the crazies now, you know. It's like a modern day St Luke's, and we all know what happened there. I'm not going, you can't make me." I pictured the scene when Mom had had one of her many 'episodes' that occurred so frequently near the end.

That was it.

It was something of a local legend, that place. It had been closed down years earlier due to reports of patient neglect or something. But that had been years and years ago, way before Dr Mellick had been practicing. Unless he was some sort of ageless monster who never changed his appearance, like a vampire or some shit. No, of course he wasn't, that would be ridiculous. As ridiculous as talking skins, though?

I read further.

There were lists of names with strange symbols next to them, or maybe they were just his doctor's handwriting. It appeared as though this was some kind of secret code that only the good doctor could interpret. It all seemed so strange.

"What are you up to?" I muttered.

There was a knock at the door. I jumped, creasing the pages. I closed the book and shoved it back into the safe as the door opened and Anna's friendly voice chirped at me.

"How you getting on in here? We were a bit worried you'd got lost or something." I turned to face her and smiled. She was inspecting the room as though it was some sort of forbidden place she'd never had access to. "It's nearly time to leave, Trevor. You manage to sort the notes? I hope you didn't fall asleep," she chuckled.

"No, no. I mean, no I didn't fall asleep and yes, I've got

the notes. I'll be out in a minute."

"Well hurry up, we don't want to have to lock you in here all night." She closed the door.

I grabbed a piece of paper and a pen then quickly scribbled down the address to the old hospital. I didn't know whether it was still standing, but the Detective in me was ready to party. Was I really planning to go there? Would he even be there? I couldn't really answer those questions if pressed, my head and body were hurting too much. I forced the piece of paper into my pocket then closed and locked the safe before placing it carefully back in the bottom drawer. I kept the keys and the pen. These would look good on the floor of the lockup, just in case the police happened to be visiting. Perhaps not the best pieces of evidence available, but they would have to do. My head was throbbing too much for me to be any more inventive right now.

SIX

I sort of knew where I was going. Somewhere deep in my sparsely filled mind was a memory of this place, this old hospital for the insane. I'd driven for about half an hour, taking a few wrong turns, but as I drove down the empty and dark road where large trees sprouted giant, menacing fingers above me, I was sure I was close.

What the hell was I doing here? My gut was screaming at me that this was where I needed to be, though. Why? I didn't have a clue.

A domineering wall guarded the grounds of the building. A large metal gate, well-worn and rusted, stuck its ancient chest out to ward off any intruders. Leaves and branches were doing their best to conceal this intimidating entrance. As I passed it I strained my neck to try and see inside. My view was blocked by the shadows from the trees, their blackened branches dancing like fingers. Were they enticing me inside or warning me to leave them well alone?

I decided to pull over a few hundred yards up the road and walk. Luckily there was a patch of wasteland with evidence of more than a couple of picnics decorating the land like a terrible piece of modern art. I killed the engine and rubbed my temples. The headache was creeping back. The pills were running low but I wanted to go in there semi-sober so took only one. If I concentrated enough I could ignore the vicious throbbing.

Staying hidden from the road I stumbled through the mud and the trees, shielding my face from the contorted branches that tried with all their might to halt my progress.

I came to a brick wall, perhaps six feet tall or so. It would be a struggle to climb, although I wasn't *that* unfit. But someone was looking down on me that night, or probably *up* considering what I had done and was planning to do. A section of the structure had collapsed. The remnants were scattered at the foot of it like brickwork innards. The wall had certainly seen better days. It was an easy climb, although as my feet made contact within the hospital grounds I was panting. Come to think of it, it wasn't the exertion that had caused my breathing to speed up like this.

After battling through a few more trees and thick roots that fought their way to the surface, St Luke's Hospital came into view. It dominated the landscape. The gothic architecture screamed of a place that you really shouldn't be visiting, especially alone *and* at night. Surely a building designed and built for housing sick people should look a bit more, I don't know, *nice?* Although perhaps when it was built this kind of crazy design was all the rage. My knowledge of architecture and building-fashions isn't that great.

A howling wind blew my hair into my eyes and the building groaned at me in mocking pleasure as I pulled my jacket closed. The walls were grey, yet most of them were covered with furry moss, seemingly the only life here. The moon illuminated the scene like a beacon of otherworldly light.

There was something shimmering in the corner of my vision that blurred as my eyes watered from the wind. It was just creeping out from behind the far corner of the hospital. A car. I'd have recognised that shiny black Mercedes anywhere. It seemed that Dr Mellick hadn't been sick after all, well not in the 'missing work' sense, anyway.

As quickly and quietly as I could manage, I headed to the opposite corner of the building. There was a door there. I'd never seen one so big, and this wasn't even the main entrance. I pulled on the handle and the cold metal sucked at my hand. The door was locked, of course. I slammed my shoulder against it and the bang that emanated carried across the empty grounds behind me. A couple of birds fled from their safe haven of a tree branch. Surely someone, Dr Mellick, would have heard me. But it was no use getting scared and leaving now. I felt far too into this to back out at this stage.

The door didn't budge. The pattern on the old wood seemed to smile at me. *What a pathetic creature trying to break me down with his puny shoulders*, it said, probably.

There was nothing else to do. The windows a few metres down were blackened with dirt and their wooden frames rotten and mouldy. I'd never smashed a window before. Despite my recent forays into murder, dismemberment, and anticipated fabrication, I'd been a pretty decent member of society, all told. But now breaking and entering could be added to my list of infamous accomplishments.

It was easier than I thought, it happened just like in the movies. My elbow throbbed from the impact, but the glass broke on the first strike. I would have put this down to my own brute force, but it must have been the old window frames and glass, and I'm big enough to admit that.

I climbed through, catching my hands and knees on some shards of glass, but the pain didn't register. This was an important mission, although the exact reason for it was still unknown. But here I was.

The broken glass crunched under my boots, the scraping on the tiled floor made me shudder. The sound reminded me of Veronica's voice. I took a few quicker paces to get myself clear of the aftermath of my entry, but it seemed that the whole floor was covered with similar pieces of debris.

The corridor appeared endless and a wind suddenly shot through the place like an arctic storm. The walls were adorned with crumbling plaster and old wallpaper that had peeled off, resembling accusatory fingers pointing at the hapless wanderer.

I coughed away the rotting smell that crawled up my nostrils like a decaying insect. The sound bounced off the tired walls, amplified as it raced away down the corridor. I halted, waiting for someone or maybe some*thing* to come rushing towards me. There was heavy breathing all around. As my breath clouded before my eyes I realised that it was me. I tried to take in a lungful of air to calm myself, but the atmosphere was too thick. I attempted the breathing exercises Dr Mellick had shown me, but at that moment I couldn't remember them. I had to get moving, though, I couldn't break in and just stand here all night like some frightened little kid.

The corridor eventually ended at a large atrium which was presumably the old reception area, judging by the large desk. The glow from the moon crept inside through the glass above the giant main entrance. The reception desk was teeming with bugs and my presence there seemed to excite them from their monotony of chewing on the old wood. They swarmed around my face and I swatted them away as though I was having a fit. Did I smell *that* bad? Even though the place was like an igloo my brow was moist, my armpits clammy and my shirt wet under my jacket. My breath dispersed slowly into my surroundings like a smoke machine.

There were dried leaves scattered around that turned into dust as I stared at them. The floor tiles were broken and soiled with dirt and what may have been old congealed blood. A couple of gurneys lay rusted on their sides, their limbs bent as though they'd been attacked and left to die in this hell-hole. Their metallic bodies were covered with spiders webs that appeared as masses of grey hair.

I listened again. There was something in the air, and it

was loud enough to cancel out the throbbing in my head. But I could make no sense of it, couldn't even describe it if I had to. I *really* wanted a couple of pills, but my inner strength advised against it.

The large staircase seemed like my only option as the other doors off the atrium were chained shut with rusty locks. It wasn't even worth trying them.

A sound danced its way through the musty air from the top of the stairs. A sort of muffled moaning perhaps? Unfortunately there was only one way to find out what it was.

I crept up the stairs as quietly as I could, but the rubbish that littered the steps crunched under my feet. Pieces of rubble tumbled downwards, making a huge din that screamed out to whoever or whatever was up there that I was on my way.

At the top of the stairs was a waiting area with rows of chairs that had once been uniformly arranged. There were chunks of plastic missing from the cheap seating and yet more of the leaves surrounding their decrepit metal legs.

The moaning grew louder and now I could pinpoint from which direction it emanated. Corridors stretched to the left and right of the waiting area, in much the same state as the one downstairs. Although littering the floor up here were bags of soiled bandages and yellow boxes on their sides, spilling dirty needles and small glass bottles.

Perhaps I'd just stumbled into a crack den? Down these ominous corridors would be rooms of junkies with belts around their arms and needles hanging loosely from their drug-infested veins. Maybe that was the reason Dr Mellick had come here. He was just helping them out, giving them morphine or something, his way of trying to do the right thing.

These thoughts were vanquished as I sucked in a deep breath.

"No, nooooo," groaned a voice. It may have been female, it was difficult to say. But it was coming from the mouth of someone in great terror. It came from the far end of the corridor on the left but was getting louder. The screams crescendoed as though whatever was at work was inflicting great damage.

It would have been the manly, saviourly thing to do to storm into the room, destroy the evil monster, and rescue the fair maiden in distress. Although it obviously wasn't a fair maiden, I probably wouldn't be able to defeat any kind of monster in my current mindset, and I wasn't feeling particularly manly. So I did what any 'man' would do in my situation. I hid.

I slipped inside the first room I came to. The moonlight from the window seemed to illuminate nothing and cast only shadows. As my eyes tried to adjust to the darkness that enveloped this place, the room became blacker still. I carefully closed the door, not looking behind me and keeping my ear against the glass. I listened to the screams from along the corridor. They became louder and more grief-stricken.

How long had I been waiting there? I didn't know.

What was my new plan? I didn't know that either.

My toes wriggled, itching to be part of the team that carried me fleetingly out of this building and back to my car, back to reality. This place was surely only a thing of nightmares.

My eyes began to allow my brain to witness where I was. There was a bed with ripped, dirty sheets in the corner of the room. A brown sink with a portion of porcelain missing stood opposite. I stared back at the bed. There was something on it.

Fuck.

A dead body.

There it lay, face down, its back slimy and shiny, reflecting the dim light. Its limbs had been arranged at right angles to the torso, the hips obviously broken, making the body resemble a bloody letter 'H'. It was then that the smell hit me. That rancid stench of decay clung to me. It was ingraining itself into my skin and rotting through my body, infecting my insides. I was on the verge of hurling as I realised what was missing from the corpse. Its skin.

"What are you doing here?"

I stood motionless at the sound. The wheezing voice was in my ear and I was too terrified to even contemplate fight *or* flight. It was much more a case of *fright*.

"Answer me," it said.

I took an eternity to turn my head. My muscles fought back in defiance, but I was the one in control, or so I hoped. And there it was, what I'd sort of expected all along.

The skin shivered before me, ghost-like in a cloud of shadows. It didn't give me a second to answer before it attacked. It flew at me like a rabid bed sheet in the wind, and although that description may sound a little comical to you, as it made contact with me all sense of comedy vanished.

It knocked me to the ground and the back of my head smashed into the broken tiles. My hair was suddenly warm and wet. The thing pounced on top of me, forcing its crispy fingers into my mouth. Oh, the taste! Imagine licking the boots of a plague doctor, you know, all the infection-filled pus and necrotic tissue of the afflicted, and you're not even close. The fingers were clasped around my tongue, my taste buds having no chance of escape. The crusty surface sliced into my tongue like a million tiny razorblades. I kicked and writhed on the floor. The thing wouldn't budge. I felt like a dog trying to free itself from under a wet blanket.

I gasped for air whilst trying to hold down the contents of my stomach but it was no use. The beast was suddenly coated with the thick spray of acidic sludge as it erupted from my mouth. It loosened its grip from my tongue but before I had time to relish this small victory it was pulling hard on my bottom lip. The inside of my mouth stretched and blood filled my mouth like a broken water pipe. The tissue ripped, my lip disengaged from its face.

The involuntary scream that came was more of a gurgle. I wondered whether I'd see my life flash before my eyes, as I was surely on the verge of death here. I closed my eyes and seemed to lapse into a state of acceptance. My cries halted and my muscles relaxed. Suddenly everything seemed so warm and peaceful.

A white light blinded me and in it I was sure I could see the silhouette of Mom walking towards me, her arms wide open and welcoming. Oh how I missed her. I tried to replicate her pose, ready to feel her warm embrace after so long. Then I saw her face.

There was anger in those once-peaceful eyes. Her mouth opened and she snarled at me, her arms now waving ferociously. "What the fuck are you doing, Trevor?" she yelled. She'd never cursed in her life. Something was definitely wrong here.

"Well?" her voice shrill and accusatory, "you're giving up, you should never give up. Remember why you're here. You are finding out the truth. Now stop being such a fucking pussy and kill this bastard. Now!"

Then she vanished. I was back on the floor with my lip being torn off, but my breathing remained controlled and steady. I slowly lifted my arms and reached out, inserting my thumbs into the skins empty eye holes. The flimsy, fleshy face crumpled like a paper bag in my hands. I pulled with every last piece of will and strength I possessed.

I must have been given super powers from somewhere. The thing tore in half with a vicious ripping sound. My lip pinged back into my face as I tossed the two halves to the floor.

My chest throbbed and my lip tingled. The skin monster lay in two pieces a few yards from my quivering body. There was no movement from it but I stared at it for an age just to make sure. I couldn't move. The exertion spent every ounce of energy from me and I teetered on the verge of passing out. My breathing showed no sign of slowing. I wondered whether I was about to have a heart attack. My mind raced, ready to shut itself off from the horrors it had just witnessed.

I opened my eyes. I was pretty certain I'd been unconscious for a while, but the darkness still reigned outside. I wiggled my fingers and toes. Yes, I was still alive. The skin remained lifeless next to me.

I took a deep breath. I had to get out of this place.

SEVEN

I stumbled forward on legs made of jelly, crashing into the door in a manner of anything but stealth. The handle jammed as I depressed it but with a forceful shake it finally clicked open. I fell, panting into the corridor. The eruption of powder from the dead leaves on the floor brought on a fit of uncontrollable coughing.

Struggling for breath I stood and looked left and then right. Shit. I couldn't remember the way out. Both directions seemed identical. I was on some kind of deserted psych ward that lasted forever.

I wiped what I thought must be vomit from my lip which hung loose from my face like a wilted flower. The back of my hand was smeared red. It wasn't vomit after all. The tangy taste of sick and dead skin made me gag. I spat a glob of chunky mucus on the floor.

I attempted to run in the direction I was sure must be the way out, but my right leg was dead from the battle. My boot scraped along the floor as I hobbled away from the screams that suddenly erupted from deep within the bowels of the hospital.

I kept on going, past so many doors I'd have lost count if I'd been trying to keep note. This corridor was never ending. The desperate moans and cries were getting louder.

Every muscle I owned seemed to ache and I whimpered pathetically as I clung to the wall for support. The plaster came away and dust surrounded me like a ton of rotten flour. Covering my face I continued on.

Whatever plan I'd had when I entered here had disappeared without a trace. The only plan now was to get back outside. But still the end of the corridor and the staircase was nowhere in sight.

My body screamed at me for some respite but I did my best to ignore it. I retched, but there was nothing inside. I hunched over with my hands on my knees and a dribble of blood splashed onto the floor. I didn't have time to inspect the wound with my fingers, it was time to move again.

The screams were deafening now. I was sure that if I turned around the source of the anguish would be standing behind me with its mouth pressed up against my ear. I lashed out just in case that were true, but only caught thin air.

I stumbled along. If only I'd have just stayed at home, maybe found another whore to add to my evidence against Dr Mellick. But in this instance hindsight was a useless thing.

I'd been trudging along the abandoned corridor for what seemed like hours but I was still no closer to reaching the stairs. I collapsed to my knees. The tiredness was winning.

"What the fuck is this place?" I asked myself, the one person I knew didn't have a clue. I rubbed my face, smearing blood all over it. Then something grabbed my attention.

The shadows along the corridor were moving. The dark forms floated like silk against a strange, ethereal illumination. In seconds they were twice the size, then even bigger. They were fast approaching. I jumped to my feet, the adrenaline kicking in despite my weariness. I turned to run but halted in my tracks as yet more of those ghastly things approached from the other direction. I was trapped.

There was nowhere else to go. I limped into the room

I'd collapsed in front of and slammed the door shut. Through the grimy glass I saw the darkness congregating. These things weren't merely shadows, they were floating skins.

In a panic I looked for something I could use as a weapon. There was a rusty bed in the corner of the room, luckily there was no skinless corpse on this one. A shard of metal stuck out from underneath, part of the frame that had rusted many years ago. I launched myself and grabbed it, feeling the rough surface break the skin on my hands. I pulled. The bed groaned but the metal was firmly attached.

There was scratching at the door. The leathery monsters moaned as they sought entry. I pulled again. The bed shifted towards me as I yanked on the bar with everything I had, but still the metal wouldn't give. The scratching became louder. I felt the bar move slightly as something on it sliced through my hand. The blood made my grip slippery but I held on with increased determination. Yes, it was starting to give. Glass shattered behind me. My ears throbbed with the ghastly sounds of the skins invading them. They would be inside in any second, ready to grab me and tear me apart like wild animals on a hunt. The metal grinded and shifted a fraction. I was getting close. The door blasted open, the encroaching sound unbearable. The army of these skins was almost on top of me and I thought I could feel their rancid breath on the back of my neck.

I screamed and gave one last yank on the metal. The bed sank with a loud clunk as the bar finally came free in my bloody hands. In an uncontrolled motion I swung it around in a large arc, catching one of the skins somewhere. It ripped but didn't go down. The room was full of them, the horde of leathery, bloodthirsty ghosts gathered around me. There was no way I could fight them all.

The window.

I lifted the metal bar high above my head and swung again. The glass smashed easier than I anticipated and I stumbled forward. I gave not a thought to how high I was or what was underneath me. I leapt from the window into the cold night air.

For the second time that evening I felt grateful for whatever was trying to help me, as a large bush cushioned my fall. My face and hands were slashed with thorns but that was much more desirable than becoming the victim of the demonic floating skins.

I crawled from the foliage like a crazed animal and stumbled to my feet. All pain ceased and the scene that had just played out was shushed by my mind as it made sure that escaping these beasts was the number one priority.

I ran. Thinking could wait.

I didn't remember how I got there but I was suddenly back at the felled wall that had aided my entry to the hospital grounds. I kept going through the trees until I finally made it back to my car. Thank fuck, it was still there.

My spasming fingers made hard work of opening the door but once inside I slammed it shut and slid down the seat into an uncomfortable ball in the footwell. I peered out of the steamed-up window. Nothing was following me.

It was then that my wounds began to make themselves known. My hands throbbed with a vicious stinging and my legs ached like the muscles were melting. My chest was on the verge of exploding and my head pounded like my brain was trying to escape.

After what seemed like hours of screaming and moaning I managed to calm myself. Just enough to notice the car headlights a little further down the road.

The Mercedes departed slowly from the front gates of St Luke's. It seemed Dr Mellick was retiring for the evening.

"What the fuck are you up to in there?"

EIGHT

I called in sick the next day. It wasn't a lie. But was I sick in the head? I wasn't entirely certain of the answer to that.

I sat at the kitchen table trying to arrange my thoughts on my next move. What was Dr Mellick up to at St Luke's? His car was there so I'd assumed he was, too. But where had he been hiding?

The skins. The seeds of my plan had been planted when I'd started looking through that textbook he'd lent me. Anger and resentment had been the overriding emotions when I'd decided that he needed to suffer for what he'd done to me. What he'd done to Mom. Back then I hadn't really thought too much of the specifics of my actions. It was as though the textbook had been some kind of instruction manual that Dr Mellick had wanted me to follow. I suppose it would be ironic that the very book he'd recommended would be his downfall.

"He's been doing the same." I shot to my feet as I said the words. In that instant everything became so very clear. Yes. He had been influencing me. He knew what I was like, where my head was at. He'd been my GP my whole life, so giving me a gentle nudge in a certain direction to suit his own needs would have been easy. Did he foresee me killing those whores? Perhaps.

But more shocking was the fact that he'd been doing the very same. In the empty rooms of St Luke's, Dr Mellick had been murdering and flaying countless victims. He was creating his own army, but for what purpose? To destroy me, to frame me for murder in exactly the same way I was doing to him?

I sat down again, these were crazy thoughts. I took a couple of pills. As my breathing became more relaxed I pictured last night in my mind.

What had happened? Did I really break in to a derelict mental hospital and get attacked by dead skins? I could picture the mass of them approaching. The smell of rotten meat licked at my nostrils. Their murderous groans muffled deep in my ears. I could even feel the metal bar in my hands. The crusty, sticky hands that now throbbed as a savage reminder.

This had to be some kind of elaborate nightmare. What were the side effects of the pills I was taking anyway? I'd never checked and I certainly didn't remember Dr Mellick telling me of any. But I'd only taken one last night, hadn't I? Maybe that was the problem, withdrawal symptoms or some shit. There'd been crazier things happen to people on medication, hadn't there?

My body shouted at me via the aches and pains that this was no case of my imagination playing games.

Yes, it all seemed real enough, even with the drugs clouding my rationale. What the hell had I got myself into? Was this all really worth it? And what did my so-called plan entail anyway? The elaborate framing of a doctor who I held responsible for the death of my mother? She may have died anyway, I didn't know. I'd gone from a kind of normal person, albeit one with a fascination of morbid shit, to a killer and a sick artist. Was this really me? All of this just to get even with someone? It all seemed a bit extreme now. My lust for vengeance had clouded my judgement and would probably end with my arrest.

A voice from deep within my mind tried to placate my actions.

You know it's all him, he's the reason she is dead. He is the rea-

son she suffered so much, especially at the end. Yeah, you don't know the specifics, but that look in her eyes whenever she mentioned him, whenever you suggested making an appointment with him for some kind of pain relief or another diagnosis. It was fear in her eyes, fear and disgust. The way he made her feel is something that no man can expect to get away with. He needs to be punished. You are doing the right thing.

I nodded my head in agreement, ignoring the pain. I'd come this far and I was damned if I was going to stop now. That bastard had to pay and there was only one way I knew how. He couldn't just wash his hands of all the shit I was going to throw in his direction. He was already up to something anyway, what would a few more corpses matter to the police?

He would pay.

The voice was quiet now but I felt it flowing fresh life through my tired body. I found the energy from somewhere to make it to my feet. I reached into the pocket of my jacket that I was still wearing and held up the bottle of pills. There were only three left. Another full bottle resided in the drawer upstairs, but it wouldn't last too long at this rate. I needed more. If only Dr Mellick would stop with all this *I'm sick* bullshit and make it into work. I was sure I could cover my contempt for him enough to have him write me another prescription.

I swallowed another pill and rinsed my face with cold water. I looked awful, but my lip appeared better already, as though it had miraculously healed itself. The cuts on my face were barely noticeable.

I'd been given a new found power. I was ready to continue my quest.

NINE

"You're a quiet one, honey, everything OK?" said Chantelle as she sat in the passenger seat. She was right, I was quiet tonight. I'd picked her up earlier and been full of bravado, but now I was driving, my thoughts whirred like a crazy mind-tornado.

"I'm just really excited," I said.

"Yeah, well tell your face," she snorted. "What's your name, honey?"

"Tre—erm, James. James Mellick. I'm a doctor."

She laughed. "Well you sure as hell don't look like one." She glanced over her shoulder at the mess of fast food containers on the backseat.

Chantelle lit a cigarette as I rolled up the shutters. The clanging of the metal was deafening in the still and gloomy atmosphere. "Welcome to my man-cave."

"Hmm, it'll do I suppose."

I walked inside and heard Chantelle following close behind. The place was empty and silent apart from her heels clicking on the concrete floor.

I threw back another pill and waited for the show to begin.

"Hey, *hey.*" Those were the only words that escaped from Chantelle's lips before the screams began. In seconds she was silenced and I heard her body slump to the floor like a sack of potatoes. I sat on the table behind the partitioning wall and pushed my fingers deep into my ears so that all was recognisable was the rapidly-beating pulse in my head. I scrunched my eyes tightly closed, waiting for it all to be over.

Something stroked my face and instinctively I threw my head back. Three ghostly figures stood before me, their empty forms glistening in the light. I'd expected it, of course. But seeing them there, like privates awaiting command from their superior officer, made my stomach churn.

"So you're finished then?" I said as I lowered my head. I watched my boots swinging back and forth, as though I was trying to run away from this whole situation.

Was I in too deep? When you ask yourself this question about anything it usually signifies that *yes, you are* and, un-lucky sucker—there's no turning back now.

"You seem distressed." The distorted, gravelly words were spoken in stereo.

I stood, ignoring their voices and strode towards the closed shutters. In my periphery they floated like black-ened angels but said nothing more.

Chantelle's skinless body was on the floor. In full Jesus Christ pose it lay, its bloody tissue twinkling in the light. Credit to the skins, they'd made this one quite the comedy piece. The whore's ears were placed over her tits, and her eyeballs and tongue were arranged on her glistening red forehead like a cock and balls. It seemed exactly like the kind of thing I would have done. But I couldn't laugh. I couldn't even acknowledge to them that I approved.

"What is the point of all this? It's not gonna bring Mom back." I was speaking to no one in particular. "Will I really feel any different once this is all over with?" A dry hand caressed my shoulder and slid down to my chest. I hadn't the strength or mental energy to resist. Then they were all having a go, feeling my body like I was some an-cient Emperor with his posse of concubines.

"Please, leave me." I was crying. Whether the tears were for what had happened here, or for Mom, I didn't know. But it felt good to cry. It felt like my mind cleansing itself of the horrors I had witnessed these last few days.

Outside I closed the shutters and rested my head against them as the tears continued to flow. My shoulders shivered and the howls of despair made me sound like a little boy. I stood there, alone until I could compose myself yet again.

My BMW's brakes squealed in pain as I pulled up outside my house. Dull streetlights only partially illuminated the silent, nocturnal road. I'd been driving for hours but my mind was blank as to where I'd been. I needed to sleep, but this seemed counter-productive. By being asleep I wouldn't be trying to figure things out like I was trying to now, I'd be allowing my subconscious to take control. That didn't seem like a good thing to do.

As I approached my door, key in hand, a gentle creak shook me from my tiredness. My front door was open.

The lock had been smashed, splinters emanated from the doorframe like wooden innards. The door slowly swung inwards, the shadows enticing me inside.

Shit. A break in. That was all I needed right now. I glanced up and down the street to check if anyone was around. The wind caressed my cheeks and brought no sounds of life with it.

I'd never been broken into before. To be honest I didn't have much worth stealing. But something inside me yelled that this wasn't just a random coincidence. Were they still inside, waiting for me? I gripped my house key between my knuckles in case I needed a weapon then tentatively stepped over the threshold.

Inside, someone was whispering.

TEN

"Trevor." The ghostly sound drifted around me like it was coming from the walls and ceiling.

The house was in darkness and I didn't dare turn on the lights to alert anyone to my presence. Surely the voice was in my head. I had no pills on me and although I was desperate for one to try and get my head together, I didn't have the courage to wander upstairs.

With my fist-key armed and ready I crept towards the living room. "Trevor, in here." I strained my neck to look inside but could see very little in the darkness. I panted, only then realising I'd had my breath held all this time.

The voice came again, chanting my name like an ancient, celestial mantra. It surrounded me and was certainly not coming from the living room.

I retreated and made my way along the hallway to the kitchen, watching my step to make sure I didn't stand on anything that would cause a noise. It was difficult, the place had turned to shit since Mom died.

The kitchen was also empty, apart from the week's worth of washing up still piled in the sink. The key cut into my flesh as my grip intensified.

"Trevor, there's no one here."

I spun, certain that someone stood right behind me. There was no one there.

After a few moments I came to my senses. The voice

continued but my tired mind was able to block it out. I checked every room silently until I was sure I was alone. Once satisfied I turned on the bedroom light and lay on the bed.

I closed my eyes.

"Trevor, listen to me."

"Mom?" It was her voice all right. Now somewhat more relaxed on the cold bed I realised it had been her the whole time. It was just her body that was missing.

"I can't do this anymore," I said with a sigh, holding back the tears.

"You can. You must, and you will, Trevor." I was reminded of being in trouble as a child, such was her tone.

"None of this is going to bring you back."

"No, but he needs to suffer."

"But this all seems so wrong, am I even going to get away with any of this?" I pleaded, still in child mindset.

She paused. "Of course, dear. But you need to do one more thing." I said nothing and instead tried to concentrate on steadying my breathing. "Trevor?"

"What, what do I need to do?"

"You need to kill him."

I sat up, eyes open and fully alert. "*Kill* him? No, I can't do that."

"You seemed to have no problem killing those vicious little sluts did you?" Her voice made me wince.

"But that was, I dunno, *different*. I had no connection with them, they were just..." I couldn't bring myself to use a derogatory word for them. I was beginning to feel something akin to guilt.

"One day, Trevor, and that shall be soon, you will discover the truth about the Great Dr Mellick. He is a poison, a cancer. He needs to die and it needs to be you who does it. My dear boy, my darling, precious boy, this plot of yours is admirable but it will never work, not really. You think you can outwit a doctor? He may be a despicable human being, but he is smart. He would easily worm his way out of any accusations you threw at him. No, he needs to be silenced forever."

I looked around the empty room and pondered what my mom was saying. She'd always been so loving, so generous and warm. She'd been my rock, the only person who ever meant anything to me. And now here she was, encouraging me to murder someone, a doctor no less. My head was spinning like I was drunk.

True, I'd been happy enough to murder in the name of framing him, but to actually kill him myself?

Although *had* I actually murdered anyone? Wasn't it the skins who were responsible? It seemed ridiculous, but I'd seen them and their work with my own eyes, hadn't I? But then who had made the skins? Was it Dr Mellick this whole time, was he the one framing *me*?

I had so many questions and no answers for any of them. I reached for the drawer and grabbed my last bottle of pills. I took two and immediately felt better.

"Mom? Are you still there?" Silence answered me. I lay down again and waited for the medicine to cure me completely.

I couldn't do it. I knew him and although the hatred I harboured for him was at a critical point now, I just didn't have it in me to take his life.

Poison. A cancer. Those words reverberated around my head like a swarm of blood-thirsty flies. Mom had never spoken of anyone in that way. As I replayed her voice in my mind my fists clenched at the thought of him bringing such vitriol from Mom's mouth.

No, he wasn't going to die at my hands. He would die rotting in prison for the abhorrent crimes he had committed. The plan would work. Although not her intention, Mom's motivational talk only inspired me to continue with what I was already doing. But now I was ready to embrace my calling.

ELEVEN

I was surrounded by floating flesh. Rotten fingernails clawed at my face and leathery hands explored my naked body. I felt myself becoming hard, ready to explode. Something began to fellate me. Even in dream-mind I was aware of the sensation of my cock being rubbed viscously with a dry flannel. But I couldn't wake up. I moaned, although not in pleasure, and writhed on the bed as the dream controlled me. I murmured for it to stop, my groggy voice having no authority here as the thrusts became quicker and harder. And then it happened.

I awoke screaming, my body sodden with sweat, and my crotch sodden with something else. I am embarrassed to admit it but yes, I'd dream-spunked. I couldn't remember the last time I'd done that. The thought made me retch and my stomach told me to get to the bathroom quick. I tried to leap out of bed but misjudged it and ended up in a pathetic heap on the floor instead. My stomach didn't let me off, though. I hurled its contents onto the carpet. I collapsed into the burning pool of liquid with tears in my eyes and cum in my pants.

This was a new low, even for me.

The shower worked its magic, though and twenty minutes later I was clean, changed, and ready for work. Today I had a purpose. It was time to notch things up on the framing-the-doctor scale. I didn't even worry that the lock on the front door was still broken. But as I said, there was nothing of any value in my house.

I breezed into work, smiled enthusiastically at my colleagues, and even wished Veronica a good morning. I apologised for my sickness the day before and promised that I was feeling much better. It was the truth. She scowled at me throughout, rolling her eyes and shaking her head. But it didn't phase me.

Dr Mellick was still off sick, which was typical. I could have really done with a backup bottle of pills. But I was yet to take one today, my new found motivation was overriding any notion of the headaches and the madness.

"I need to just check some of the patient notes in Dr Mellick's surgery," I said to Veronica, "didn't manage to finish up the other day. Is that cool?"

"Fine, I'd prefer you away from reception anyway. Just make sure you actually finish this time." She stormed off, already huffing and ready to lay in to someone else for leaving a dirty coffee cup on the desk, or something else equally trivial.

I powered up Dr Mellick's computer. While the system booted up, which took ages, I opened the filing cabinet and safe, then laid his notebook on the desk. I opened it with clumsy fingers to the page where the address of St Luke's was written. I hadn't noticed before how shaky and almost nervous his handwriting was. Perhaps if someone were to, I dunno, write more there, it may seem as though it was from the same hand. My hands were shaking anyway, but more out of excitement than nerves this time.

I glared at the words on the page, my throat clenching. I tried to swallow but my body seemingly wanted me uncomfortable as I had this realisation.

Trevor King.

Why was my name there? Was I on his list, soon to become a floating skin in the deserted hospital corridors like those other luckless fools?

That fucking bastard.

My body shook as I read my own name over and over again. A few deep breaths calmed my nerves and I read the words once again. My rage melted, determination now taking centre stage in my thoughts. A smile crept over my face. I couldn't let my emotions own this situation. If I was doing this, I needed to be in control.

The computer pinged as the home screen flashed on. I opened the word processing programme and was greeted with the password screen. But this wasn't a problem. In the back of the notebook were a few usernames and passwords and it didn't take me long to find the correct pairing.

I sat back in the frankly very comfortable seat and took in a breath. I didn't really know what I wanted to write here so I simply relaxed my mind and began typing, hoping that the words would just flow. I was grateful that my anger had subsided.

I've had this compulsion for so many years I cannot even begin to recall the time that it commenced. Working with the human body is a great gift that has been bestowed upon me, and the intricate workings of the systems have always been a huge fascination of mine. Whilst training, oh so many years ago now I don't like to think, the thing that always grabbed my attention and stimulated my mind was the practice of dissection. It wasn't a morbid attraction to death, of course, more so it was the exquisite beauty of the human body. In death you can stare in wonder at life. The muscles, the bones, the organs, the fascia holding it all together, the very nature of what makes us alive. The removal of the layers to reveal the workings beneath them was like discovering the magic of our wondrous existence, like unwrapping the most magnificent birthday present. I would stare for what seemed like hours as the lungs were dissected to reveal the intricate structures of the bronchioles and alveoli. Or the kidneys and liver which showcased intricate details of the subjects' lifestyles. But what was always most fascinating to me was the skin and how it could be removed so easily. Our largest organ, the one that encases and protects all others is such a weak and malleable structure once the life it preserved inside has gone. There is something so poetic and tragic about that.

I was trying to sound 'doctor-y' but for someone un-medical like myself, it didn't read as such. Perhaps Dr Mellick was a little 'out of his mind' when he wrote this. Yes, that was it. I decided to rank up the psychopath.

One day, when my work is discovered, I hope that those who find it shall not judge me too harshly. For all I ever wanted was to explore what makes us truly alive. We should not be scared or frightful of these wonders, perhaps basking in the art that death can provide will open our souls and minds to another level of appreciation.

I was losing my thread by now. But what I'd written so far was a start. I dated the document two weeks previously and printed it out. I made sure not to save it to the hard drive as this was something I couldn't see him doing. And the fact that it would be saved with today's date would certainly rouse suspicion. Shit, I might as well sign it myself.

I took the paper from the printer, scuffed up the edges slightly, and placed it in the safe before turning my attention back to the notebook.

I grabbed a pen and practiced my shaky handwriting on a piece of paper. After a few attempts I was satisfied that it looked enough like Dr Mellick's.

Underneath the address of St Luke's I wrote the street where I'd picked up the whores, and a few hooker-sounding names, including Alectra and Chantelle. I even referenced that textbook he'd lent to me, for a bit more evidence.

I checked the clock. I'd been over an hour in here so I put my incriminating words back in the filing cabinet and shut down the computer. I snuck out of the office like a ninja, even if I do say so myself, and returned to reception to continue with my working day.

TWELVE

My recent exertions were catching up with me. As I drove slowly along Victim Street my whole body ached immensely, as though my muscles were attempting to stop me entirely. But instead of cursing or whining about my injuries, I considered them part of the bigger picture. None of this was going to be easy and a few battle scars were to be expected, perhaps even cherished.

It was too early in the evening for the hookers to be out, I still had a good hour at least. I contemplated going home for a while but the thought of Mom appearing again, if she was ever there in the first place, kept me away. I didn't want another argument.

I pulled over and rubbed my tired eyes. As the street around me flashed and blurred, all I could see in my mind's eye was Dr Mellick's smiling face. It *must* have been him who had broken into my house. Was he looking for me, or just trying to scare me? My mom had told me I was alone, but then she's dead and I've never been the clairvoyant type, not to my knowledge anyway, so how could I believe the words she'd spoken? Sorry, the words I'd *believed* she'd spoken.

But worrying about whether the spirit of a deceased parent was trying to communicate important information to me was the last thing I should have been thinking about. I was convinced that Dr Mellick was on to me.

That's why he hadn't been at work. He'd been busy concocting a monstrous scheme to bring me down.

The thought then occurred that perhaps he wasn't alone when he had broken in. Had he brought his skins with him? Were they there to try and destroy me for good this time? I shuddered as I remembered the rough, crinkled skin I'd ripped in half, and the desperate scratching on the door as they tried to get to me in St Luke's.

This was war. If he was recruiting his own army then I would do the same. My lust for vengeance was strong enough to have my minions die for me.

My thoughts began to run away with themselves. I had to concentrate on the here and now. I was here for a reason and was not yet ready to abandon my plan at the first sign of danger.

A dirty, hunchbacked bum stumbled along the pavement beside my car.

"Hey, buddy, how's it going? You having a good night?" I shouted as I got out, attempting my best friendly voice. The bum didn't appear to hear me, or assumed I must be talking to someone else. I jogged to catch up with him. "Buddy?" I tapped him on the back.

"What tha fuck ooo wan'?" he grimaced as he glanced over his shoulder. He was so taken aback he nearly dropped his bottle of Value Brandy.

"It's me, James," I said. The knotted eyebrows displayed confusion on his grimy and haggard face but I continued anyway. "You remember, from the park?" He was homeless, surely he must hang out at the park.

"Yeee, I remember yooo, frm th' parr," he mumbled and took another gulp.

"You want some more brandy, bud?" I nodded at his booze with my eyes wide.

"Shurrr, I's wan' shum b-randy, maan." His eyes lit up. They were staring at me from behind the mass of grey beard that adorned his face like a hairy rash. His breath hit me more potently than I'd anticipated and I stepped back, blowing the rancid odour back at him.

"Come with me then, I got lots." I signalled to my car. He didn't need to be told twice.

Luckily for me, and my car, the lockup wasn't far away. The windows were open and the cold air whisked across our faces, but it didn't hide the smell of decade-old body odour, rotten food, and shit. Not even close. I made no small talk and neither did he. He was too interested in his brandy. That suited me just fine.

My work was going well. After escorting Buddy inside the lockup and listening to the terrified, yet drunken screams, I returned to the pick-up point. I managed to bag two at once; Kandi and Crystal. They giggled like school girls in the back of the BMW that seemed to be rattling even more than usual tonight. Once they entered my kill room their laughing ceased immediately.

I popped a couple of pills and lay on the table. The shutters were closed but a cold draught surrounded me. I could hear the shuffling of the skins, like disciples congregating around their master. They said nothing, but I knew they were listening.

"I must commend you on your fine work. Your numbers increase. I think we are ready to pay Dr Mellick a visit."

Six floating skins was not quite the number I'd had in mind, if I was being totally honest, but it would have to do. It seemed as though time was getting seriously short. I could not delay things any further.

My eyes remained closed as the woozy feeling from the pills descended upon me. "We are here for you," said a collective of soulless, wheezing voices. I smiled. My troops were ready for battle.

My confidence was at an all-time high. This was the night when it would all end for Dr Mellick.

THIRTEEN

The skins were laid out on the backseat of my shit-piece Beemer like expensive garments incongruous to their surroundings. They reeked of decay. Part of the smell was probably the remnants of Buddy after he accepted my offer of free brandy. I suppose I should have treated the skins with some kind of preparation to stop them from rotting, but I didn't know of any. Perhaps the textbook mentioned something, but I'd mostly been looking at the pictures. Formaldehyde, was that something?

The skins hadn't moved since I'd picked them from the floor and transported them to the car. I told myself they were simply conserving their energy for the confrontation that I expected to materialise once we got inside the old hospital. Surely the presence of the evil Dr Mellick would rouse them from their slumber. Something in my gut insisted I would be seeing him tonight.

I trudged through the trees, the skins slung over my shoulder like multiple soldiers wounded in battle. I moved with steady caution to prevent them catching on any of the branches. I made my way over the broken wall and stood in the shadows of the guardian trees, staring at St Luke's Hospital.

Dr Mellick's Mercedes was again parked where it had

been the other night. He seemed to be a creature of habit. Doctors always like to have their own private car parking space after all.

I entered the building the only way I knew how, through the broken window. Once inside I laid the skins out on the cracked, soiled floor.

"Come on then, wake up." They remained still.

Maybe I needed some special incantation to reanimate them, but I was damned if I knew one. That sort of information was probably not included in Dr Mellick's textbook.

Confident the skins would awake when needed I left them and walked silently down the shadowy corridor. Had I visited this place in a previous life? I felt like I'd always been here, so natural was my journey to the main foyer and the grand, old staircase. The windows creaked as the wind thundered against them, threatening to crack the glass; the old wooden frames warning me to leave this place as they groaned like lost souls.

But I couldn't leave, not now. He was here. I needed to see him. I'm sure he expected me, too. He knew I was on to him and he would stop at nothing to be the victor in this sick game.

I threw back my shoulders, took in a breath, and began my ascent. There was a swagger to my gait. I had all the gusto of some viking entering enemy territory, ready to kill their men and fuck their women. What would my viking name be? Trevor the Terrible, or Trevor the Tormentor, or something.

But I wasn't ready to announce my presence with a war cry just yet. I was still assessing things. The place was exactly as it had been last time. At the top of the stairs the waiting room was still covered with dry, dusty leaves. I checked down both corridors; right and left. There were no strange shapes floating towards me. Either they were unaware I was here, or were simply waiting for me to make my move. I wondered whether Dr Mellick had found the skin I'd destroyed the last time I was here. Did he feel sadness, or was it just another motivating factor for him to –

A scream raced along the corridor. A gust of wind threw me backwards and I stumbled, but remained on my feet. The source of the scream disappeared, but the echo still bounced from the walls and reverberated inside my head. My bravado dried up instantly. I glanced behind me to make sure I wasn't being followed by any of those beasts. Alone.

"Get a grip of yourself, Trevor. Don't you back out now, pussy." My words of self-motivation were heeded.

My boots crunched on the debris, causing unwelcome noise. My tentative steps did little to silence it. A door slammed from behind and it's echo surrounded me, violently dancing along the filthy bricked walls. I froze and listened. From somewhere further down the corridor was a muffled cry. I collected myself and took another step.

The sweat was dripping into my eyes and I shut them tightly before drying my face with my sleeve. The silence engulfed me once more.

The wall appeared out of nowhere, I'd reached the end of the long corridor. I looked back to try and make sense of it. I'd walked further than I thought. The brickwork before me had been painted white but years of neglect had darkened its colour significantly.

I turned again, not believing what my eyes had just told me. The corridor flashed in and out of focus and I had to reach out to steady myself. My palm met a door, an unlocked door that creaked open with the pressure. Suddenly all thoughts of the fuzzy corridor disappeared as I stared at the horror inside the room.

The room was illuminated by the moon piercing the grimy windows. My first thought was that it was a naked woman sitting in a chair, who displayed the remnants of a, how can I say, rather heavy period. I recoiled at the sight.

But this was no woman. The lack of tits, and the hairy chest and legs cemented this realisation. And then the cause of all the blood became apparent. The man's crimson cock lay between his feet like an infected maggot.

The body was magnetic. The sight disgusted me, yet it pulled me inside the room with its invisible force. It dared me to investigate further.

The man's head was flopped back, exposing a deep gash in his throat. A similarly deep, but much neater laceration emanated from below the mortal wound and continued to the bloody mess at his crotch. His hands were behind his back and his legs tied to the rusty chair legs.

The door slammed shut behind me, making me jump. I turned around.

It was Dr Mellick. Dressed in a black suit and matching tie, he smiled at me like a proud father.

"Very good, very good indeed." He clapped his hands together, his *bloody* hands, and approached me.

I stepped back, catching my heel on the victim's foot then losing my balance and instinctively reached out to steady myself. My hand slid into the warm and slimy wound between his legs. I pulled my hand back and felt a nausea vibrate inside. I gagged. Funny how other people's murders and mutilations seem to disgust me so much.

"You are getting better at this, Trevor my boy," said Dr Mellick, turning his attention to the bound body. "I have to say, I am very impressed."

"What the fuck are you talking about?" I said as I frantically wiped my bloody hand on my shirt. "Are you insane?"

"*Me?*" he laughed. "Oh, Trevor." He walked behind the dead man, his stare never leaving me. "What have you got yourself into here? This isn't you, is it?" He kept his pace around the corpse.

I mirrored him.

We circled the body with our eyes locked.

"No it's not, you crazy bastard. Who is this guy?"

"I didn't know him, did you?"

He was trying to fuck with me and granted, it was

working. I tried to reply but my tongue locked and I just mumbled some incoherent noise. "What are you doing here?"

"That is a question only you can answer." He stopped walking. So did I. "You brought me here, Trevor. I don't know why but I'm sure you had your reasons, however deluded they may be."

I still couldn't respond, my mouth was suddenly dry and try as I might, I couldn't work out how to swallow.

"You seem a little lost for words. Perhaps your actions should do the talking, no? Are you going to make a start with this one? You've made your markings, you know you'll have to make haste if you are to remove it properly, *professionally*."

"What?" I really did have more to ask, like why did he think that it was me who had murdered this man, cut off his cock, and made a ghastly incision along his body? But my throat defied me.

"Trevor, this is getting us nowhere. Come on now, do what you have to, it is your plan after all."

My voice returned. "What do you mean, my *plan*? What do you know of a plan? I came here looking for you, and here you are, more of a sick fuck than I ever imagined."

Dr Mellick held up his hands and showed me glistening red palms. "Please, all this acrimony will get you nowhere. You're an artist, Trevor. Please, make your art." He nodded to the corpse with a look that suggested I knew what he was getting at. My silence and frown told him I was in the dark, though.

He removed his jacket then rolled up his sleeves, sighing. He approached the man and carefully inserted his fingers into the laceration on his chest. He got a sturdy grip as the wound squelched with fresh blood that trickled down the body.

"I really didn't think that you'd be getting me to do this, you know. But I suppose it's the way you're working now, getting your employees to do your dirty work while you stand back and take all the credit." He pulled at the flesh forcibly, yet carefully and it began to come free. He squirmed his fingers further along, releasing more of the man's skin from the tough fascia beneath.

"What are you doing?" I said, a sickened intonation in my shaking voice. But why was I asking? I'd already witnessed the fruits of his labour first hand. Would he get this dead bastard's skin to try and kill me, too?

"Trevor," he was now peeling the skin free like he was helping the man remove a wetsuit, "you know exactly what I'm doing. Have you not read my textbook? Page 33, it's going to be a tricky one but I'm quite sure it will be achieved."

I tried to retrieve the page from my cloudy memory. I had studied the book in detail and now recalled the piece he was referring to. The tendons had been severed and the body laid out on the floor with the muscles flowing like a number of demonic-looking wings. In the textbook the picture had looked like the body was mid-flight. When I'd regarded it, I'd never thought in a million years I'd be able to replicate it. It seemed Dr Mellick was more confident in his ability than I was in mine.

When I stepped back, having reminded myself of the details of page 33, Dr Mellick had already placed the body on the bloodstained floor. The muscles resembled the ribbons on a maypole; twisted and shiny, as though they were trying to escape their cadaverous tomb. Behind it hung the skin like a pig in a slaughter house; gutted and ready for chopping.

"I admire your skill. You're a fast worker, you have obviously had plenty of practice," I said, which was a strange thing to speak when watching such a deplorable act. Yet as the words resonated in the room I realised that it was Dr Mellick who had spoken them. He was standing in the corner with not a flicker of emotion on his gaunt, dark face. His sleeves were rolled down and his hands were clean.

I looked down at my now bare and blood soaked arms and stumbled forwards. I fell against the freshly removed skin, hanging before me like a museum exhibit. It wrapped itself around me like a warm, sticky blanket. I fought to free myself but the job was much harder than you could imagine.

Finally ridding myself of the flesh garment I sunk to my knees and ground the heels of my bloody hands hard into my temples.

"Why are you doing this to me?" I whimpered as the tears began. Even after everything I'd just witnessed, all I could think about was Mom. I pictured her lying in bed, her skin pale and looking like she was already dead. Her bony fingers tried to hold my hand but there was no strength left in any part of her.

I sniffed back the tears and stood with a new found vigour. The doctor watched me from the corner of the room. He didn't flinch, not even his eyes flickered as I marched up right into his face.

"You fucking killed my mom, you piece of shit," I spat at him. Not even my globules of saliva brought a reaction. I watched them gleam on his wrinkled face like incandescent pus-filled spots. He continued to look me in the eye, then cleared his throat and took in a breath.

"Is that what you really think?"

"Yeah, it is." It wasn't much of a response, certainly not the way I'd pictured this scene going.

"Trevor, your mother had an inoperable brain tumour. It wouldn't have made any difference had she received treatment. I am sorry to have to tell you this."

"You're *sorry*?"

What did I really expect anyway? Was he going to laugh at me and tell me how he knew she'd die, and that he had the power to change things but didn't? I'd genuinely believed he would break down and admit his fault in her death. I was sure he'd come clean about how he'd held her life in his hands and through either choice or negligence, had been the one responsible.

My shoulders drooped in a sort of defeat and I looked at the floor. He shuffled his stance, only briefly, but there was something in the way he manoeuvred himself, some subconscious tick that told me he was lying. My gaze returned to his eyes. And there, deep in the dirt brown pools of sludge in his eye sockets, was a sparkle. His lips moved into a semi-smirk and his face relaxed. It was the look of a guilty man.

"Well, I'm sorry, too," I said. I threw my arm back in a flash then thrusted my fist towards his smug, murdering face.

I imagined his jaw splitting in two, his tongue severing and a shot of molten blood erupting from where his mouth used to be. That would have been a satisfactory sight for my vengeance-fuelled eyes. But my fist never made contact.

Something grabbed my arm. I turned to see what but was suddenly thrown across the room. My head slammed into the wall and I whimpered with the terrorising agony as it spread throughout my head. My fingers tingled and my vision became blurred. Somehow I spied the skin of Dr Mellick's latest victim storming towards me. Its gait suggested violent intent but I had no energy left to try and escape. Dr Mellick had gone, or perhaps he was hiding in the shadows. The door opened with a creak that pierced my ears and a group of the skin beasts entered. The floating silhouettes were blood-hungry.

I closed my eyes, expecting the end.

FOURTEEN

Was I dreaming? My eyes showed me images, my ears played sounds to my mind, my body ached and my head throbbed. But something about the whole experience was, I don't know, *off.*

I staggered to my feet, the floor was wet and sticky. A breeze cooled the sweat and, I'm sure, the blood from my brow. A leathery ghost fluttered in the shadows.

Noise surrounded me. It sounded like a war zone. Violence and death. Terrified cries, screams of triumph, howls of defeat. The sounds were coming from outside in the corridor.

I shuffled forwards, not daring to look back. From the corner of my eye I was aware of the skinless corpse arranged on the floor. I had to get out of here, and not for the first time.

The corridor was murky, with plumes of dust congregating before my eyes. I wheezed and coughed, it sounded like my lungs had the bass turned up to 11. I waved my arms to try and rid the fog from the air but it did nothing.

I ran.

The screams intensified as I progressed down the corridor. The doors to the many rooms off the hallway were now open and from inside came voices whispering my name through the din. But there was no sign of Dr Mellick.

A hand gripped my shoulder but with a sharp shrug it vanished. Even if I was being followed the atmosphere made it near impossible to see anything. I glanced behind me and one of the shadowy skins floated amongst the dust. It reached out an arm. The fear ignited my pace.

The floor of the waiting room at the top of the stairs was littered with what looked like scraps of paper. But when I looked again it was actually skin. Brown, wrinkled skin. It had been torn apart and I remembered the time I'd ripped one in half in this very hospital. What the fuck was happening?

"Trevor, come quickly." The voices echoed around me. No, it couldn't be. Was that Alectra? Buddy? My army? For a brief moment I saw the six of them on the stairs, their arms flailing in an attempt to guide me. But as I reached the stairs, the fog digested them into its depths.

I bounded down the stairs. Then I was sprinting towards the exit, the broken window, when something tripped me. My face slammed into the floor and for a split second I was convinced I'd broken my jaw. The sensation quickly passed and, moving my jaw with my hand, I stood.

My body was pleading with me to rest. Fire pumped through my veins, acid engulfed my muscles, my lungs pumped like a steam engine. I leaned forward and tried to compose myself.

"Trevor, watch out." The voices were too late with their warning, though.

A mass of cold, wrinkled arms engulfed me, throwing me to the floor once again. Then they were on top of me, a pile of rotten, putrid blankets. I clawed at them with every last piece of energy I still had. But I was weakening.

Is any of this real? Was the inner voice my own? It sounded like me but I was in the wrong mental and physical state to assess it.

I couldn't go out like this, killed by the skins of Dr Mellick's victims. Was he too much of a coward to do it himself?

No, it wouldn't end this way. Some primal survival instinct suddenly kicked in.

The skins exploded from me as I punched and kicked my way to freedom. In seconds I was on my feet and scampering towards the exit from this terrible place.

The skins moaned, the breeze from their movements fresh on the back of my sweaty neck. Their screams nestled into my ears but I didn't slow. It was as though a horde of giant insects was descending upon me. I did my best to ignore them and remained steadfast, concentrating on nothing but the broken window.

I howled. The burning in my legs was threatening to set my trousers on fire. The window wasn't getting any closer, in fact it appeared to be shrinking into the distance. But still I kept on. The leather monsters reached for me, making contact but gaining no purchase. With windmill arms I lashed them away from me.

Suddenly I could feel the cold air from outside as I finally neared the window. I collapsed to my knees and crawled through. The feel of the concrete on my fingers brought delight, although my hands were bleeding as the shards of glass sliced through them.

Something gripped my ankle. I jerked my foot but it didn't let go. It pulled at me and I began to retreat back inside. I dragged myself forwards, feeling the muscles tear in my arms, and roared in defiance. The hand loosened with a satisfying ripping sound.

I never looked back. I stumbled across the grass to the trees and then the wall. I had to get back to my car. My heavy breathing alone, nothing followed me. The thought to check for Dr Mellick's car never entered my mind. I had to reach my own.

I slammed the door shut and clicked the locks closed. Sitting there, panting for dear life, I surveyed my surroundings. Alone. The skins hadn't, or couldn't, follow me.

A few moments later my breathing slowed and I fully realised I'd escaped. I smiled.

"Nice try, fucker."

FIFTEEN

Dr Mellick's dark brown eyes stared at me through a haze. His laughing echoed around me, the painful sound of his joy penetrating deep into my mind. "I killed your mother. I watched her die," he cackled.

I brought my arms up and tried to make a fist, but my muscles refused the order. I pathetically attempted to reach out and strike his smug and mocking face but he seemed to dodge each of my weak attacks. My throat burned as I tried to scream that I was going to kill him, to make him pay for what he did. But his laughing only grew louder and my arms retreated from trying to hit him, and instead tried in vain to cover my ears from his incessant and sadistic sniggering.

My bedsheets were wet as I awoke with a start. I was alone and as I held my breath to listen, the silence that greeted me was alarming. I stared at the ceiling and only then realised that it had all been a dream. All of it; the hospital, the skins, the revenge. It *had* to have been a dream. How could it have been real?

I sat up, on the verge of being sick. The throbbing from the back of my head was intense, like a ghost was punching me relentlessly in one specific spot. I relaxed carefully back onto the pillow. It was sticky. It wasn't just sweat that was pouring from my head. I remembered being thrown across the room while Dr Mellick stood and watched. The memory was nothing like that of a dream, and the injury to my head was testament to the fact it *had* happened. All of it.

That murdering bastard.

After a few minutes of lying in the darkness, I shuffled myself to the edge of the bed and slid to standing. I took a pill, unsure if they were actually doing anything anymore. It seemed that the headaches and the madness followed me whether I was medicated or not.

I took a breath then slowly stepped out of my room and across the landing to the bathroom. The piss flowed out of me like fire water as I sat on the bowl with my head in my hands. I felt like I'd been out drinking again and before I knew it was coming, the sick was in my mouth. I had no time to reposition myself on the toilet and instead hurled between my feet. The liquid sizzled as it hit my boots and pants. I groaned that hangover groan that never makes you feel any better. The pill I'd taken was still intact but dissolved rapidly in my pool of vomit. Perhaps that was a sign to lay off them for a while.

I headed downstairs, the place was freezing. My front door was wide open, the lock still smashed. I needed to get a locksmith out soon, but it was the last thing on my mind. I grabbed some aspirin and washed them down with two pints of ice cold water. I hobbled into the lounge and lay on the sofa. I closed my eyes.

"I killed your mother," said a voice. I leapt to my feet, gasping for breath. There was no one there. "I killed your mother," it said again and I realised that it was all in my head. That bastard had not only killed her, he was also driving me insane. I glanced at the mirror above the fireplace and Dr Mellick's face smiled back at me. His mouth moved rhythmically with the words in my mind. I stood and stared at him, daring him to continue as I tried to keep my balance.

"Fuck you, *fuck you*," I cried as my fist crashed into the glass. The mirror sliced the knuckles and blood seeped over my hand and down my arm. The doctor's face vanished, but I continued to punch with both fists anyway. My hands were numb after the fifth strike but my arms burned as though they had been dipped in acid.

I picked up the armchair with a bout of superhuman strength and threw it against the wall. The paper ripped and plaster dust rose forth like a cloud of cigarette smoke. It caught the back of my throat and I coughed uncontrollably, which only made me more angry.

"Fuckin' bastard shit motherfuckin' fuck," went my mantra, or something like that. The armchair, lying upside down with a broken wooden leg, smiled at me. It gave me that same smug expression that Dr Mellick had when he mocked me from the mirror. I kicked the chair, breaking another leg, then pounded at the fabric with my fists, turning the cream covering a slimy red.

"I killed your mother," whispered the chair as I beat it like a crazed animal. I kept on going, my chest becoming tight as I struggled for breath. "I killed your mother," it repeated with no sign of letting up.

Eventually I fell to the floor in defeat. But the voice never relented. I filled the air with profanity and screams doused in both anger and despair, trying to silence the incessant mocking in my head. Unable to stand, I crawled from the living room. The trail of blood I left behind me looked like red slime excreted by some kind of giant slug.

I made it to the kitchen where I managed to pull myself up using the table, and sat on the hard dining chair. I banged my forehead on the table, hoping that the force would quiet the voice in there.

When I awoke, sitting at the table with my head pounding and my fists stinging, it was dark outside. The house was in silence which was only broken sporadically by cars driving past.

"Mom?" It was the first word that came to mind, one

to test my throat with. Of course there was no answer. I looked at my hands, they were a mess but the blood was beginning to clot in blackened lumps, which was the tiniest of mercies in my present state.

What was I going to do? I wasn't safe here. Dr Mellick was sure to come back. He had done so before, breaking in while I wasn't at home, maybe he'd come back again and finish me off.

I stood and opened the cupboard, taking out the bottle of Jack Daniel's which was fuller than I'd thought. In little over half an hour it was empty. Half an hour after that I fell asleep again in a booze-fuelled and pain-soaked stupor.

SIXTEEN

I was in no fit state to go to work, but I had to. Even if they sent me home straight away I had to at least try and see Dr Mellick. Surely he'd be back in today.

The drive in was, in a word, *agony*. How I didn't crash I'll never know. What were the police playing at, letting someone drive through rush hour traffic like that? There were numerous car horns and gesticulating hands directed at me, but I really was in no mood to try and retaliate.

I'd half-expected the stares from my colleagues to be the most shocked yet, but as I walked behind the reception desk I didn't even receive a glance. The air had a subdued aroma to it this morning.

My makeshift bandages were already seeping with fresh blood. Extending my fingers to try and log in to the computer brought a pulverising sensation along my hands that shot up my arms and burrowed into my shoulders.

Anna sat down beside me and leaned in to whisper. "Have you heard?"

What, how Dr Mellick is breeding an army of skins?

I looked at her, expressionless. "No, what's happened?"

Anna shifted her seat closer, she had the excitement of someone in-the-know of the latest gossip. "It's Dr Mellick." She said the name in slow motion, at least that's what

I heard. My gaze darted, making sure no one was looking at me and my reaction to Anna's words. Was she staring at me with accusation in her eyes? "He's missing."

"Missing?" I spluttered, "what do you mean he's *missing?*" My chest tightened and I felt my cheeks flushing. Was she on to me? Were all of them?

"Well, we all assumed he was sick, he'd called in after all." If she was trying to play it cool she was doing a damn fine job. Although if she were this good an actor surely she'd not be working here. "Only, we don't think it was him who called." Anna leaned back with her eyebrows raised, letting the statement sink in.

"I don't understand," I said. It wasn't a lie.

"His wife called this morning, said he's been missing for days. She assumed he was away on a conference or a meeting or something, so thought nothing of it at first." That seemed weird. "I don't think they're all that close to be honest, not anymore." That sort of explained it. "Anyway, when she couldn't get in contact with him she phoned the police and reported him missing. She phoned here this morning and spoke to Jill over there. When Jill told her that he'd called in sick, well, his wife got all crazy on the other end, calling him all sorts. Didn't sound like he was the loving father and husband we all thought he was."

I'd never thought that anyway, I almost said.

"Excuse me, Anna," I said as I laboured to my feet, "I just need to check something." She seemed a tad upset I wasn't prepared to listen to any more of her tale, but her ringing phone soon put her back in work-mode.

A mini-scandal such as this was a perfect opportunity to escape and sneak back into his office to investigate further. Although on this particular day, I wanted to do nothing of the sort. My head hurt, my hands hurt, my stomach hurt. Shit, it would be easier to list what *didn't* hurt. I'd taken a couple of pills on the way in and they should have been working by now. It seemed I wasn't ready to ditch them just yet.

I needed to do this. I was so close, as I'd been telling myself for quite a while now. It was time to stop wallowing.

The notebook was as I'd left it in the drawer. I slammed it on to the desk, not meaning to do it so violently, then returned to the filing cabinet. There were piles upon piles of paper in there, creased and folded in a way suggesting they weren't all that important. I rifled through them like a predator pulling apart its prey, hoping that I'd find something, *anything* that would explain what he was up to.

Had he been here? Was he still at St Luke's? Had he visited the lockup or even returned to my house? The answers surely wouldn't be here, but I knew I was close to learning something.

"That's it," said a voice in my head, Mom's, as I picked up a pile of letters bound by a crusty elastic band. I turned, expecting her to be standing behind me. Of course she wasn't. But I wouldn't be alone for much longer. I needed to work fast.

I took the letters and sat at the desk. As I removed the rubber band it snapped with a tiny plume of dust. There were sealed envelopes along with loose letters. Each of them displayed that barely recognisable scribble, a poor excuse for handwriting that could only belong to a doctor.

My stomach whirled as I read the name and address that was written on all of the envelopes. Even in that handwriting I could see it as clear as day. It was an address I knew well.

"Mom?"

I dropped the letters, my red-bandaged hands shaking. It couldn't be. Why was he writing to her? They didn't know each other, apart from a doctor-patient relationship. Doctors never usually wrote to their patients like this. My intrigue turned to anger. What the fuck was he saying to Mom?

My mood calmed slightly as I realised, obviously, that

these letters were never posted despite having stamps attached. The stamps were old, though. The corners were upturned and gnarled, and the prices on them were certainly not the current price of stamps, far from it. The envelopes were stained brown, the markings signalling years of neglect in a locked drawer. Were these even written to have ever been read?

"Open it." I wasn't sure whether it was the voice in my head or the one from my throat instructing me to do so. Whichever it was I wasn't going to argue. I had to know what this piece of shit wanted with my mom. I tore clumsily at the envelope and removed the letter, which I'd inadvertently ripped in the process. Then I read.

Dear Sheila,

Please believe me when I say how truly sorry I am for everything you have been going through recently. The last thing I ever wanted was to make you unhappy. I do so hope that you believe me. You have brought a great joy to my life these last few months and this I will never forget. I never dreamed I could have these feelings for anyone else, and to share them with such a kind and beautiful woman as yourself has been an honour I am simply unworthy of.

But I think you know that this situation is one neither of us can afford to pursue. I have a wife and two young children, if they ever found out about us or the baby I think it would destroy them. I admit my love for my wife is not what it once was, but it is still love and the sacred bond of marriage is one I have always intended to keep. I cannot leave my family over this. Yes, I've been a fool, but haven't we both?

To put this in a letter is cowardly, I know. But I cannot bring myself to look into your eyes as I ask you, no, beg you to do the right thing. It is still very early, it is not even really a life yet, just a collection of cells. No one will judge you if you decide to do what's right. I have friends, they can be discreet. It is a simple procedure these days.

It went on for pages. Excuse after excuse on why she needed to get rid of her baby. *Baby*? No, this had to be some sick joke. Mom and Dr Mellick? I didn't believe it. What would she have seen in him anyway? Was she his bit-on-the-side, some sordid mistress he kept secret from his failing marriage? My stomach constricted. Mom was no one's mistress. Lies, all lies.

But it seemed so genuine. The more I read as the paper quivered in my fingers, the more it seemed to sink in. How could she have been so stupid?

I put the letter on the desk after skim-reading the latter part, I didn't want to hear any more details or excuses on why he was such a fucking bastard. I thought about Mom. What a terrible time that must have been for her. She'd never mentioned it to me, probably blocked it out for all those years. Being forced into having an abortion was something I'd never really understood, not having a womb. But the stories I'd heard and TV shows and documentaries that dealt with it had shown me what a terrible ordeal it was. Poor Mom.

I wiped a tear from my eye with a bloody hand as I pictured her in those final days, dying in her own bed in a foetal position of horrific pain. I wondered whether the procedure she'd gone through back then had been as terrifying.

I composed myself somewhat, then picked up the letter again. My mouth hung open. It couldn't be. The letter was dated eight months before I was born.

"Fuck."

SEVENTEEN

"What the hell are you doing in here, Trevor?"
I dropped the letter from my shaking fingers as Veronica yelled at me from the doorway. I didn't respond, I didn't know how to.

"*Well?*"

She walked over to me and shook my arm. The pain this forced down into my hand was excruciating and I howled, pulling myself away from her. I stood and faced her, my head sunken.

"What is all this?" she demanded, eyeing the letters on the desk with drops of fresh blood adorning them. "Why are you going through Dr Mellick's papers?"

I looked into her eyes, there was hatred in them. My mouth opened but no words came out. I stood there mouthing air like a fish as Veronica sneered, shaking her head.

"Is there something wrong with you? Are you actually *insane?*" The word sliced through me like a rusty dagger and I juddered. "I mean, *look* at you," she sneered, appraising me up and down, "you're on your last warning, Trevor. I don't know what's been going on with you these last few days, well *weeks* even, but you had better get yourself together, sharpish!"

She glanced at the letters, papers, and the notebook on the desk like she was watching a horror movie. "How dare you go through all this, what are you hoping to find exactly? And what's with all this *blood?*" It was as though the word sickened her. "Dr Mellick is missing, his wife is in bits, and all you can do is go snooping through his things. This is disgraceful behaviour. After everything he did for you? I never wanted you working here but Dr Mellick had only high praise for you and convinced me to take you on, more fool me. What would he say if he could see you snooping through his possessions?"

Something suddenly snapped in her. "That's it, forget final warnings. Get out of here, *now!*" Although she'd been a pretty consistent bitch throughout my whole time employed here, I'd never seen her so disgusted in me before. It was as though I'd been going through *her* things, and bleeding all over them.

"What do you mean?" I said, finding my voice, though it now sounded more like a whisper.

"You're fired. Get your things together and get out of my sight." She was actually shaking and the sweat was glistening on her wrinkled forehead. "Do I need to repeat myself, Trevor?"

I held my hands up, my communicative skills returning to me when they were needed most. "Wait," I took in a deep breath, "I know where he is."

Veronica rolled her eyes and folded her arms. "Do you *really?* And where is he then?" She stood there with a half-smile half-grimace, like a mother waiting to hear the lame excuse from their child about how they *hadn't* broken that precious ornament. "I haven't got time for this, not today, Trevor. Now I want you to stop all this—"

"St Luke's Hospital," I interrupted, which didn't impress her, "that's where he is."

A smile eventually cracked her lips before she shook her head to rid her face of it. "The abandoned hospital? And why on earth would he be there?"

"I can't really say too much, it would sound too – weird." Veronica smiled, she actually seemed to be enjoying this, witnessing the insane ramblings of someone who had just been given his marching orders.

"Too weird, huh? And why would it be weird? Please tell me, Trevor, I'm all ears."

"The thing is, I think Dr Mellick is into some strange, well, alternative medicine may describe it. I was concerned he may be hurting people so the other day I snuck in here and went through that drawer in his filing cabinet." I glanced at the drawer in question, Veronica followed my gaze. When she looked back her face was even more incredulous.

"Go on."

I flicked to the right page and found the address of St Luke's in the notebook. "Look," I said, holding it up for her and ignoring the pain in my knuckles. "Here." Veronica regarded the page with a frown, arms still folded. "I don't know why, what it meant to me, but somehow I just knew that was where I'd find him. So I went there, the other night, I went looking for him. But what I found there was too terrible for me to describe."

"Try."

"You would never believe me. I think we need to tell the police, though." Was it time to bring the police into this? I'd said it without thinking about the consequences. But now I'd made the leap and would probably have to roll with it.

"Tell them what, how some deranged psychopath who works in a doctors surgery had a gut feeling where a missing doctor had vanished to? Don't talk ridiculous, Trevor. I really think you've said enough."

"There are other things, too," I said but she didn't want to hear them. It was a relief, though. I wasn't ready to put into words the discovery I'd just made. Veronica had made up her mind about me long ago and I wasn't about to change that now. The bitch didn't deserve to know about

Dr Mellick being my... No, I still couldn't admit it, couldn't *believe* it.

"Clean this mess up and get the hell out of here. I don't want to ever see you here again, do you understand? You won't say any goodbyes either. You shall walk through that door and never come back." She turned and left, slamming the door behind her.

I cried. I didn't know why. Was it Mom, the truth I thought I'd discovered, or losing my job like this? It didn't really matter. I stood with tears dripping from my eyes and blood dripping from my bandaged hands. What a pathetic creature I must have looked.

I sat down at the desk and rubbed my eyes in the hope that it would cleanse my mind of all this shit. Dr Mellick's chair was comfortable but I'd never noticed before how it seemed to fit my butt perfectly. Was it because we were related? No, of course not. I was angry with myself for even contemplating it.

I stared into the black computer screen and regarded how truly terrible and washed out I looked.

What was happening to me?

I scratched my head and ran my fingers through my greasy hair, forgetting about the gash on the back of it. I winced as blood trickled from the disturbed scab.

I remembered the times in the lockup. The bodies, the skins, the whole bloody dismemberments. I gagged at the memories. What was I thinking? Was I really capable of all that?

But it wasn't me, it was those fucking skins. They'd murdered those people, flayed them like animals, and produced this so-called 'art in death'.

I began to wonder whether any of this was actually happening. Was I really a sadistic killer, or was I merely a vessel for these supernatural beings to inhabit and manipulate? Or was it really Dr Mellick behind all of this?

No matter the answer, one thing was certain. I was losing my mind.

Whatever had gone on was all done in the name of revenge, though. Revenge against that heartless fuck who killed my mom, and tried to make her kill her unborn child. Was it really me he wanted dead? Was he still trying to pursue this?

Murdering bastard!

"Like Father like Son," said that voice in my head, this time resounding around my skull with the deep timbre of Dr Mellick's.

"*No.*" I stared at the grief-ridden reflection in the monitor. My face smiled gently and raised its eyebrows at me.

"You know it's true, you've always known," said my reflection. "Mom was so ashamed of it all that she never mentioned it. But at the end, she tried to tell you, in her own way." My face gave me an expectant look.

I pictured standing over her in bed, her skin almost transparent and her limbs curled up like her muscles had melted. I'd stroked her thin hair from her face and wept as she'd looked into my eyes, but stared into my soul. I'd blocked this memory, until now.

"Your dad, he's still alive," she'd said. "He tried to help me, but no one can save me, not now. You might say he's the one best suited to try, but he has others to see to now. A loving wife and family."

At the time I'd put her words down to the drugs or her illness. But now, as my reflection guided me to remember, her cryptic clues in her dying breath made sense.

She died that night. She'd been in and out of consciousness for hours, and then she just didn't come back to me.

"You did work it out, though," my lips mouthed on the screen, "after they came and took her body away. You sat for hours thinking about what she said, until it all made sense. Then you started drinking. Folks were concerned for you, always there to offer their support or a shoulder to cry on, which you never accepted. They all thought it was the grief that led to the drinking, not the denial of a parent."

"Shut up, shut the fuck up," I yelled at the screen, my reflection mocking me as I did.

"Why else did he get you this job? He was looking out for you. He tried to be there for you, but your mother would never allow it. She made him your doctor for one reason only, to show him just what he missed out on. But your father embraced this chance to spend time with you, if only briefly and in a strictly professional manner."

"It's not true, I'm not his son, just stop feeding me this bullshit. Not now, not when I'm so *close*!"

"Do you really want to do this to your own blood? It's not too late to back out. Think about what you're doing."

"Fuck off, you crazy bastard, just go and fuck yourself," I said quietly. I hadn't the energy to scream anymore. The mirrored me sensed it and was silent.

I leaned back in the chair as my pulse raced. I fingered the bottle of pills in my pocket. I pulled them out and looked at the plastic container, inspecting it for the first time in a long time. Had that bastard been poisoning me? I never knew what these things were and for all I knew he could have been medicating me to do exactly what he wanted. I wouldn't have put it past him.

I threw the pills to the floor and stamped my foot down hard. The bottle cracked and the pills became a powder on the dull, brown carpet. I had no use for them anymore. I was going to do this sober.

It was then that I made my decision. For once in my life I needed to do the right thing. This needed to end.

EIGHTEEN

The police station was grim. Cold grey paint adorned the sterile walls in the waiting area where a couple of junkies huddled together while a cop talked to them, shaking his head. At the desk someone was complaining to the officer behind the streaked glass about their car being stolen. If only I had something so trivial to report.

I stood and waited patiently, fiddling with the bandages on my hands. I'd wrapped them up with fresh gauze before leaving Dr Mellick's office and they were yet to be soiled. The noticeboard to my left was adorned with flyers and public information leaflets. The papers were yellow and faded, leathery almost, a bit like...

"Yes, can I help you?" The cop behind the glass tapped her fingers on the desk, a wide-eyed expression on her pretty face urged me forward.

"Oh, hello, I..." my throat clenched. On the way here I played out the scene so many times. But now standing in front of someone in uniform, I choked. I took in a deep breath, coughed and tried to compose myself.

"Sorry about that, I have some sensitive information for you."

The cop sighed and picked up a pen. "And what is this regarding?"

"It's about that missing doctor, Dr Mellick?"

The cop put down the pen again and narrowed her eyes. "And what exactly can you tell us, Mr...?"

"Trevor, Trevor King. I work with him. Well, I used to."

"Right, and what else?"

"Look, is it possible to, you know, talk somewhere quieter?" The junkies behind me were arguing with each other, the cop who was dealing with them attempted to calm them, but was failing.

"I'm sorry, Mr King, we have a lot of people just walking in off the street with information they claim to have. If you've got something important to say then you should just say it here."

"He's my father," I snapped.

Shit. I'd admitted it, said it out loud. There wasn't even a moment's hesitation. I winced, feeling my skin crawl as it did when the skin beast mounted me and tried to rip out my tongue. I was disgusted with myself. I told myself it was simply to get her attention, and hoped this were true.

It seemed to have worked, though. "Have a seat please." She indicated the chairs over by the noticeboard of rotten skin.

"Thanks."

I sat down and watched her as she picked up the phone. She nodded then mumbled something I couldn't hear. After a few seconds she hung up and looked over at me. Her stare was hard to read. Did she suspect me of something, or was she just giving me the 'cop look'?

I put my head in my hands and stared at the floor. This was stupid, coming here after everything I'd done. It wouldn't take long for them to piece everything together. One look in the lockup and I was finished. That's if they looked there, though. If I was careful I could come out of this on top and Dr Mellick would be the one forever wearing a suit with stripes on it. Were they aware of the doctor's dark side? Perhaps that's why the cop had been so suspicious of me. Did they think I was Dr Mellick's accomplice?

"Trevor King is it?"

I jumped, as though awakening from a nightmare. Above me towered a man in a creased white shirt with his tie loose and top button open. His chin displayed fresh stubble while heavy bags highlighted his bloodshot eyes. The musty sweat on him stung my nostrils.

I stood as the man extended his hand to me. I held up my hands and shrugged at the bandages with a weak smile.

"Right," he said, lowering his hand. "I'm Detective Monckton. Would you like to come with me?"

"OK."

I followed him through a security door and down a narrow hallway. The space shared a haunting resemblance to St Luke's. Monckton said nothing, just turned around a couple of times and gave me a smile he probably thought was warm. Each time I directed my gaze to the floor.

Monckton's office was like a teenager's bedroom. The desk and floor were littered with papers and forms, with a dirty coffee cup or three next to his computer. It reminded me a lot of Dr Mellick's office. He motioned for me to sit before taking his own seat behind the desk.

"So, Mr King, can I call you Trevor?" He picked up a pen and opened a notepad.

"Sure."

"My colleague informs me you have some information on Dr James Mellick, is this correct?"

I shifted in the seat. I suddenly really needed a shit. "Yeah, right, I erm..."

"Trevor, relax. I appreciate you coming in, anything you can tell me would be a great help."

He paused and studied me. As his eyes met mine I felt as though he could see right into my mind. He never once looked at my hands, but I hid them under the desk all the same. I took in a breath, my gaze darting around the room, although nothing of note stood out to me. It was all a blur.

"Look, with all due respect, Trevor, we are very busy here. Is there anything in particular you can tell me. My colleague mentioned you are Dr Mellick's son." He glanced over a sheet of paper with scribbled handwriting adorning it. "I see no mention of him having a son here." He looked at me, his face expectant.

"Well, to be honest, Detective, I have only recently found this out."

Monckton leaned back and frowned, but said nothing.

"It's just..." I mumbled, "...that's not important right now. They were saying, at work, I used to work with him see? At the Millennium Surgery? I was on reception."

"You *used* to work with him?"

"Yeah, well, I've recently lost my job. I've had a few issues in these last couple of weeks and my mind hasn't been my own." He wrote something in his notebook. "I'm not some crazy, though," I added. He wrote down something else.

"Trevor, all I'm concerned about is finding him. If you can help me do that, great. Any problems you have been having are none of my business right now. But we can help, if you need it, or indeed want it. There are people you can talk to. But could you tell me a little of what you know?"

He didn't display any signs, but I could feel his irritation rising. The room suddenly seemed warmer. My armpits were moistening and I felt a dribble of sweat creep down the inside of my arm.

"St Luke's," the name flowed from my lips as easily as that of a loved one. It felt good saying it. "St Luke's, that's where he is. He's not missing, he's hiding."

Monckton wrote it down. "St Luke's?" he asked the air. He stared past me, his tired eyes contemplating and seemingly not for the first time today. "That name is familiar."

"It's the old abandoned mental hospital just outside of town," I informed him.

"That's right," he said, momentarily out of character

and relieved that he no longer had to work his memory centres. In seconds he'd composed himself, though. "Forgive me, Trevor, but that sounds very strange. An *abandoned mental hospital?*" The way he punctuated the words made me wonder for a moment whether I was crazy. What was I saying? It sounded ridiculous. But I was succeeding so far. Monckton was enthralled.

"I think he's quite a sick man, Detective."

"Sick? In what way? From what I've been told he is a loving husband, father, and grandfather." Monckton placed his pen on the table and linked his fingers, his eyes fixated on me.

"I'm not sure his relationship with his wife is quite what you think it is, sir." *Sir?* Why was I calling him sir all of a sudden?

Monckton rubbed his eyes. "OK, Trevor. What exactly is going on here? You come to the station, tell me how you're the son of Dr Mellick, how you've only just found this out. You then say he's hiding in an abandoned hospital, and that his relationship with his wife is, well what *exactly* are you saying about *that?*"

I knew what he was thinking. He didn't believe me, not a word. To him I was just some lunatic from the street who'd turned up with a make-believe story to try and get some attention. I was sure they were already aware of my situation; losing Mom, living on my own in the family home, medicated daily to keep whatever mental issues I had at bay. Just a sad, frightened kid who wanted the important doctor to be his real daddy. I needed to get him listening properly.

"OK, so this is going to sound strange, I'm not sure I even believe it myself, but I think that Dr Mellick has been..." could I say it? "...murdering people."

"That is a very bold statement, Trevor," he said, shaking his head with no hint of shock. "What makes you say that? Do you have any evidence?"

"I do."

Monckton held out his hands. "Yes?"

"I think I can help you. Take me to St Luke's, I can speak to him."

Detective Monckton sighed and put down his pen. "Trevor, I'll be honest, I don't know what to make of you. This does seem like a very elaborate story, don't you think? Who has he killed? When? How? These are the questions we need to answer before I'd even consider investigating the hospital. Can you see things from my point of view? These are very sweeping statements. I need some evidence."

I was losing. Did I really expect anything less, though? I'd watched enough cop shows, the gritty realistic ones, to know that he wouldn't just take me at my word.

"OK, fine," I said as I stood. "I tried to do the right thing. There's a monster out there and if you aren't going to take me seriously then it's going to look pretty bad on you when he kills again."

Monckton squinted his eyes shut. When he opened them they bore right into me beneath sharp eyebrows.

"Can I go now please?" I said.

Monckton stood, his demeanour screamed *I'm too old for this shit.*

"Wait here." He left the room, shaking his head. I sat down again and looked at my bandaged hands. There was a faint stain of red on them. I fingered the material and smiled. Things were coming together nicely.

NINETEEN

My thinly-veiled attempt at blackmail had worked better than expected. I sat in the back of the car and said nothing. Monckton was in the passenger seat, occasionally glancing over his shoulder while we drove in silence. I was just a helpful member of the public fulfilling his duty as a diligent citizen. That was the line.

He must have known they were on to something, though. Why else would he have agreed to this? Perhaps they were so short on information they'd give anything a try.

Two patrol cars followed close behind us. It seemed they were prepared for whatever eventuality was to occur at the abandoned hospital. There's safety in numbers, I'd heard someone say once.

"I think he's hiding out there, or something, to try and get away from it all," I muttered as we approached the hospital. My neck tightened and my throat clenched in anticipation, and perhaps a little fear, at what might unfold.

"Is that what he said to you?" said Monckton.

I didn't answer. It would have been stupid to elaborate now we were so close.

We pulled up in front of the old, rusty gates and the two patrol cars did likewise. Monckton ducked his head and stared out of the window. Dusk was settling over the building and the dimness brought shadows to life under the gables and window frames; the hospital watched us with a host of tired eyes.

"Are you sure about this?" he said, scratching his neck like he had a rash there.

"Yes, I am."

Monckton shook his head, sighed, and opened the door. The group of cops left me in the car for a couple of minutes while they discussed something outside. Eventually Monckton opened my door and signalled me to get out. I was surrounded by uniforms. They looked at me with down-turned eyebrows. I was unsure if they were annoyed with me for bringing them out here or whether they suspected me of something. Or maybe they were just trying to intimidate me.

Bring it on.

One of the officers tugged on the metal chains holding the gates shut. They didn't budge. "Round the corner, there's a broken wall that we can get through," I offered. The officers laughed as a tall skinhead showed me the massive pair of bolt cutters in his hands.

"No need for some broken wall when you're police," he said, snapping the cutters at thin air. What a prick.

In no time the chains were severed and the gates forced open. They creaked loudly, enraged that they were being used after so many years of rest. The metallic moan filled the air, it flowed in the wind all the way from the building. Was it a warning from the hospital?

From the gravel driveway sprouted weeds as tall as trees. They danced in the wind, directing us towards the building. We walked in silence. The wounds on my knuckles tingled.

A thick pile of leaves had blown up to the main entrance, blocking it like a brown snow drift.

"There's a broken window round the side," I said, breaking off from the group. They muttered to each other but followed.

The window was as I'd left it. I'd feared that nothing would be as I remembered it, as though I was losing my mind or something. But no, everything was as it had been. Except for Dr Mellick's Mercedes, that was gone. Maybe he was, too.

I hunched over and moved towards the window when a hand seized my shoulder. "Just hold on there," said Monckton. He pulled out a flashlight and inspected the interior of the building.

Something felt wrong. The hairs on my neck quivered as a cold draft massaged my body. I stood up straight and coughed. Everyone looked at me. I could feel their suspicious eyes burrowing into me. I rubbed my eyes, feigning tiredness.

"So this is where he's hiding out is it?" said an officer.

"Keeping the place clean for something is he?" chuckled another.

"Well let's find out," said Monckton, it sounded more like an order. The seven of us clambered through the window and stood in the long corridor.

The stench in the air was thick in my throat. Two of the officers gagged. So did I. Monckton didn't flinch.

"Straight ahead. It leads to the main entrance and the stairs," I said between coughs. The smell was intensifying.

Monckton looked at me. "Yeah, I'd figured that out. Thanks, Virgil," he replied before flashing the light along the corridor and motioning for us to follow him. Their flashlights illuminated the walls haphazardly as we walked. There was an air of caution from all of the law enforcement.

We reached the stairs. Monckton circled his flashlight before signalling to two of the officers to check the corridor opposite. They nodded and proceeded down there, muttering to each other. The door to the corridor was open, not closed and bolted like the last time I was here. This was too strange.

"He was upstairs, when I saw him," I said quietly, instantly regretting it as I saw Monckton's reaction. He was a man who didn't like being told what to do.

He led us up the stairs. The remaining three officers were scared, I could tell. They'd have blamed their shivering on the cold, but they couldn't fool me. There was no such fear displayed on the Detective, though. His flashlight guided him as he strode confidently, his chest pushed out and his eyes alert. He never once checked to see whether we were close behind.

The putrid smell worsened at the top. My snot felt like post-mortal discharge burning inside my nostrils. We stood in the waiting room with our hands over our mouths and noses, retching. An officer spilled his stomach at the stench and complained he was feeling faint.

"For fuck's sake," spluttered Monckton, "just sit down and wait here. Call yourself a police officer?" Embarrassed, the man, the *pussy*, duly obliged without a word in protest. The skinhead guy chuckled and made some derogatory comment.

And then there were four.

Monckton sniffed the air, seemingly immune to the death scent. "This way." He headed down the corridor in the direction of where I'd been attacked by the monsters the other night. I could still feel the sensation in my bandaged hands of ripping that skin-bastard in two.

I followed. "This smell's getting worse," Monckton said to himself. He was right. I was certain I was chewing on rotten meat, the back of my throat sizzled with the acrid fumes.

"You two, check down there," he pointed to the corridor leading the other way. "You," he nodded in my direction, "follow me."

It was as though Monckton had some kind of sixth sense. He passed a number of rooms, paying them no attention. I could still picture the torn pieces of skin, those beasts my very own skins had defeated to rescue me from certain death. But the open doors displayed only empty spaces. Nothing more. It was kind of fucking weird, but I suppose there was some creepy explanation for this sense of abandonment. Monckton had no interest in these rooms, though.

Then we reached the door, *that* door.

My heart was racing. Surely he was going to find the body arranged on the floor and the shredded victims. And then what? Arrest me? That seemed the likely outcome, but I couldn't run. There were five other officers in the building, all much more physically fit than me. There was no chance. My injuries, recently forgotten about, suddenly reminded me of their presence. I stumbled forwards, landing on my knees and cracking a tile with a bloody hand.

Monckton ignored me and pushed the door open with his flashlight, reaching for his gun with the other hand. It seemed to take an age to open fully, the hinges creaking like in a bad horror movie. I couldn't see inside from where I was but his reaction told me everything I needed to know. He stood frozen, his mouth hanging open.

"What the fuck?"

The eerie silence was suddenly broken by possibly the most fear-fuelled scream I'd ever heard. It came from along the corridor. The audible pain ricocheted along the walls, deafening me with its desperation. In an instant it was over and the silence regained control.

"What was that?" mumbled Monckton quietly, with no hint of appreciation for the horrific screaming. He stood motionless in the doorway with his shoulders slumped. I remained silent and he didn't press me for an answer. He just stood there staring with the gun and flashlight quivering in his hands. It was as though he'd seen a ghost.

TWENTY

Stumbling footsteps and a pathetic whimpering resonated in my ears. I glanced down the corridor to the source. The cop, the one with the bolt cutters, hobbled towards me. Gone was his arrogant smirk, replaced with the face of a terrified child. There were tears in his eyes that even the darkness couldn't hide.

Behind him gangrenous shadows began to form. They spread up the walls and ceiling like multiplying bacteria. They were gaining on him. The desperate cop's radio escaped from his grasp as though it were alive. He managed to catch it as he fell to his knees, jamming his finger on the button and screaming into it.

"Backup... St Luke's... Hurry..." That was all he managed.

The radio crackled one final time before it fell to the floor and smashed like a cheap toy. The shadows coagulated in a cloud of blackness and crept over his trembling body.

Is it too far-fetched to describe the following moments as an outer-body experience? I suddenly felt myself released, looking down on myself from the shadow infested corridor. I watched the figure that was me as it stared open-mouthed in awe at the cop and his blanket of shadows. Was this some kind of withdrawal symptom from the pills?

A floating skin appeared on top of the cop. Its fingers pulled at his jaw. He made no sound. In seconds his flesh was being torn from his face. The wet ripping was a sound I'd heard all too often before. An eruption of blood quickly followed and the cop was slammed forward, his raw face becoming one with the grimy floor.

The shadowy skin reared up like a caveman after its first kill, the celebratory cry was far too human for an act such as this. The cop lay lifeless, blood trickling from his exposed muscle and sinew. His face was ruffled at the back of his neck like a hood. His head jutted out at a strange angle, the neck broken.

My thoughts were disjointed and I had trouble believing my eyes. Had I really just witnessed this? It seemed too bizarre for my thoughts to process. In seconds the skin had rejoined its posse of shadows and disappeared into the darkness that engulfed the long disused corridors of St Luke's. The only thing that remained was the dead cop.

I stood, my mind suddenly back in my body. My fingers clicked under the freshly soiled bandages, there was blood on my jacket sleeves. Pumping out my chest and feeling my spine clunk, I took in a deep breath and looked over my shoulder.

The beam from Monckton's flashlight shook violently from inside the room. Clearing my throat I turned and strode towards the room. All of my previous aches suddenly vanished. I looked down at my bloody bandages, squeezing my fists tight then extending my fingers. I'd never felt better.

I walked into the room like I owned the place, expecting to see him still staring at whatever monstrosity was on display. For some unknown reason I felt excitement at witnessing his terror, and even more so to behold what its catalyst was.

His gun clicked.

I admit I was taken aback somewhat. I'd never had a gun pointed at me before, especially not one held by someone obviously in quite a lot of distress. Was that better? If given the choice between that or a trained marksman with me in his sights, I'm not sure which I'd choose.

His flashlight was also pointed at my head and the bright glare forced my eyes to shut.

"You sick little bastard," he wheezed. "You getting some kind of hard-on out of all this are you? I should put a bullet through your head right now, you evil fuck."

He surprised me with his vitriol. If I was able to open my eyes fully I would have given him a frowned look of confusion. Instead it was just a squint.

"What?" I said as I held up a hand to shield myself from the light.

Monckton lowered the flashlight but kept the gun on me. I squeezed my eyes shut, seeing only flashing, random colours, then opened them. It took a second or two for the room to come into focus. I was beginning to understand.

The flayed man sat in the chair and was no longer butchered on the floor. His muscles now glistened with a green ooze, his tiny cock shrivelled on the ground before him like a necrotic potato chip. The scene was horrific and the smell even more so, but I felt nothing, other than confusion at him sitting back in the chair. My gaze was now on Monckton. From the corner of my eye I saw the skin hanging behind him.

It danced in a non-existent wind. Like a crusty piece of fabric it groaned as it fluttered in the air. The skin had turned a dirty brown colour and the area around the crotch was a blackened mess. What with the perfect incision down the centre it looked like a jacket hanging up, the breasts and arms swaying back and forth as though it were trying to reach out for something. The face and hair had been preserved perfectly, *too* perfectly. The empty eye sockets watched me carefully and I recognised that look all too well. The dark holes in the wrinkled face regarded me with a kind of parental pride. It was the skin of Dr Mellick.

"Mellick," I muttered, "what has he done to you?" The voice came without my brain processing the words. It was though someone else was speaking through me. I stepped forward, holding my fingers out as though to embrace the skin of my dead father.

Monckton screamed at me. "What the hell are you talking about?" I halted and gave him an intent stare. "You just stay right where you are." He took in a breath, lost in thought. "Mills, Hendricks, get in here, *now!*"

"Oh, Detective, they're dead," the words and calmness in my voice shocked me. My heart was beating quickly but as the statement left my mouth I realised it wasn't from fear. No, this was the thrill of anticipation.

"So you killed them, too?" He was beginning to sound like he was holding it together, but his twitching arm gave him away. "Trevor King, I am arresting you for...."

He couldn't even finish his sentence. I laughed, or more specifically, I *watched* myself laugh. I actually applauded him, too.

"I'm afraid you're wrong, *Detective*. There's no way out of here, not for you. Your men are dead and soon you will be." I sounded like a psychotic murdering baddie from some 80's cop movie. "You cannot defeat us."

Monckton lowered his gun and looked at me like I'd just eaten my own shit or something. "You're fucking crazy. You brought us all the way out here, playing along like you were trying to help, and all this time you had him here, like *this?*"

Trevor, the man I was now staring at, shrugged his shoulders. "You know, for a Detective you seem awfully unprepared for any of this. Has this never happened to you before? Surely it must have done. You seem quite old, you have to have been doing this shit for a long, *long* time. Or are you just not that good a cop? I mean, you're here alone with a skin-removing psycho, aren't you?"

What the fuck was I ... he saying?

Monckton's wedding ring played a tattoo on the gun.

"You think you're going to get away with this?" He shook his head, probably realising how cheesy that line was. Or perhaps he knew that this was simply not true.

I was myself again. Monckton dropped his flashlight. The beam illuminated me from below like I was some kind of prophet. His gun arm turned white as he gripped the weapon ever-tighter, racking his brains to find some solution to his present situation.

But it was his eyes. The vessels were bright and red in the milky whites, and his pupils were growing larger by the second. The fear in them almost spoke to me. Now I remembered the looks on the whores' faces when they knew their lives were over. Even Buddy, too drunk to fully comprehend it, had known. They'd all known, especially Dr Mellick, my absent father.

Monckton brought his now free hand to try and steady the gun. He was trying to fight the knowledge that he was about to die. His survival instinct was intense, I'll give him that. I closed my eyes with an instinctive smile plastered on my face.

And then the gun fired.

TWENTY-ONE

The draft from the bullet felt like a demon bolting from hell as it flashed across my face. The gun fired again. Dust and pieces of rotten plaster fell upon me.

I was still alive. I opened my eyes.

Dr Mellick's leathery hands clamped tightly around Monckton's skull, the crinkled fingers pressing deep into the Detective's eye sockets. The cop's arms flailed and the gun flew from his grip. The muffled scream that emanated from his mouth was the sound of pathetic desperation. And pain. *Lots* of pain. The blood flowed down his face like a viscous slime as his body began to lose its rigidity. He fell to his knees but the skin fingers held on. His eyeballs popped like plastic bubblewrap. I not only heard them, I *felt* them. My cheeks were throbbing from the smile my face had constructed.

Monckton was thrown forwards where his body convulsed like a palsied seal. I wasn't sure whether he was dead but after a second his body ceased to move and the pool of blood around his head gave me my answer.

This was the only way. He'd have never let me leave here a free man.

The skin of my dead fa – Dr Mellick was as it had been moments before. It floated over its victim, almost fluttering in celebration.

When I looked back at Monckton's body it was skinless. The flesh twinkled in the moonlight. My bandaged hands were crusty but a wet layer of blood now christened them. I felt a tightness in my chest as though I'd been exercising.

As the shadows enveloped me I sat on the floor and crossed my legs. I felt woozy and was aware of my conscious leaving my body yet again.

I watched my past self as I squeezed the life out of my victims. My hands quivered as they took the lives of so many. I watched my blood-stained self-remove the skins with psychotic precision.

Trevor dissected limbs and torsos, he created his art with the fervour of a man taking great delight in his work. The images I saw were so real, it was like watching old home movies, albeit snuff ones.

But still, something felt off. I didn't believe any of it. The memories of these acts were too hazy and possibly pill-induced.

"That isn't you," whispered Mom, her words sucking me back into my own head.

"What do you mean?" The room was empty. An old, rusty bed sat in the corner with a brown-stained mattress, but my mom wasn't there. Was I actually speaking to myself?

"You're not a mass murderer, you're my boy. None of this was you."

"But it was, Mom, I understand that now. Those pills Dr Mellick prescribed, they were to suppress these inner demons, to make me believe I was a normal member of society. But they didn't stop me doing what felt natural. I've always had this compulsion, it's just that after you died I felt like I could finally act upon these urges."

"No, Trevor. I always knew you were special. It was always you and me against the world, an army of two. But please don't torture yourself with these ideas of being an indiscriminate killer. You killed only one, the one you had to."

I was taken back to our conversation when she'd tried to convince me to kill Dr Mellick, and how I'd refused. But I'd already killed him when we spoke about it, surely she would have known that.

"You are a crazy bastard," wheezed a voice, one that sounded real, unlike the angelic voice of Mom that I only heard in my fucked up head. I looked up at the skin of Dr Mellick.

"What did you just say?" I sneered at him, *it*.

"She is right, though. You have a gift, Trevor, *Son*."

I stood and walked slowly towards the floating skin. A draft blew and the arm flittered, as though he was extending it to me.

"You have no right to call me Son."

I took his hand-skin in my own and snatched it towards me. The force ripped the arm from the chest with a screeching tear. With my fingernails I scratched at the torso and head, trying to tear him into a million pieces. I howled. The sensation of his skin being destroyed brought fresh strength to my muscles. This was what he deserved.

When I entered the empty eye holes the skin pleaded with me to stop. But I was far too into this. I pulled and ripped and savaged him until he was just a mass of leathery tissue piled on the floor beneath me.

"I guess you didn't see *this* in your fucking textbook, did you?" I spat upon his remains.

The rotting body of Dr Mellick watched me from the chair. I walked towards it and kicked the putrid cock across the tiles. I remembered now the way his eyes rolled back as I sliced it from his body, and the feel of warm blood pulsating over my hands. I smelt the metallic tang in the air and felt the sticky clots on my arms. It was as if I was reliving the satisfying ordeal in all its glory. It all seemed so long ago now.

Perhaps it was because that kill meant something to me

that I remembered it so vividly. But back then I was too dosed up on the pills or in denial that I'd witnessed Dr Mellick carrying it out on a nameless body.

I was angered that I couldn't picture the other murders. At that moment I wanted nothing more than to revel in the ecstasy of taking those lives. But my mind didn't allow me to. It clouded once again as if Mom was in control of it, sparing me from the reality of my actions.

I looked at the body in the chair. "Not hung like a shire horse anymore are you, you bastard?"

I stood over the slimy excuse for a father with my fists tight beneath the bandages. I slammed one beneath the jaw which snapped loudly, before a spurt of thick, globular gunge exploded from somewhere on the face. His head deflated and wheezed as I struck it again. It felt good. I wondered whether his skin had felt the pain, or if his soul was watching me as I tormented the last of his physical being. But really I didn't care if it did.

Was this closure? Perhaps it was, or perhaps this was a new beginning in my life, free of the drugs and free of the emotional agony he'd bestowed upon me. Whatever it was, it was the end.

TWENTY-TWO

I crumbled to the floor and lay there, staring at the ceiling. I felt nothing now. No anger, no sadness, no guilt. I'd no idea if time was still passing around me, my very existence seemed vacuous.

I was a killer, with many victims to my name. I pictured Dr Mellick's kidnapping perfectly. I'd been watching him long enough to know his routine. At the time I'd blanked it out, arriving home in the early hours with no memory of my previous whereabouts. Purposefully forgetting I'd taken him to St Luke's, my spiritual home, to dispose of him. Deep down I'd known, but perhaps a part of me wanted to keep it a secret until the time was right.

The kidnapping, the torture, his murder. He deserved it all. But the others? The details still eluded my memory.

Without the pills in my system everything should have become clearer, shouldn't it? Something wasn't sitting right and no matter how hard I tried I couldn't put my blood-stained finger on it.

A sound from outside the grimy windows interrupted my reverie. At first my heavy breathing masked it, but soon it became so overpowering it was the only thing my ears could detect. A siren. Correction, *lots* of sirens.

I stumbled to my feet as the room filled with flashing

109

blue light. It brought on a hideous colour to the exposed flesh of the corpse in the chair, who's head now flopped down over the shoulder at an impossible angle. The bed in the corner remained empty and Monckton's body lay glistening on the dirty and blood-ridden floor.

Shouting exploded outside. One voice above all the others barked instructions. Then the shrill of feedback erupted. The backup had arrived.

There were screams of 'Police' and the usual shit they shout in hostage situations. I'm sure he actually said, 'Come out with your hands up, we have you surrounded,' however corny that would have been. A couple of gunshots sounded and glass smashed in response.

I shuffled to the window and watched. There were four police cars and two vans parked outside the main entrance. Masked shadow figures carrying guns ran towards the building, poised and ready to fire. I hadn't been noticed up here.

My shoulders sagged as I considered my options. It seemed there was no way out. I'd been caught. Maybe I could plead insanity, I sure as shit felt insane.

Another two cars screeched to a halt to join the ranks. Maybe the army would be here soon. It seemed I was quite the psychopath.

I'd struggle to fight them all. Best get those hands in the air, or jump through the window to my death. It definitely wasn't going to be the latter.

"Master." My breath caught as the voice behind me echoed around the room. Never before had the words felt so comforting, so *right*.

I turned. The room was bustling with skins, hundreds of them. I recognised many of the faces. The cops who'd journeyed here with me were there. Monckton was standing to attention at the front of the group, as were the multiple whores I'd seduced, and not just the ones from the lockup.

"You are not imagining any of this," said Monckton's

skin. "This is the beginning of the rest of your life. Your soldiers have obeyed and will continue to do so. You planned on framing your father for all of this, but you are the glorious one who should rightfully be taking all of the credit. He did not deserve it. We are here to serve you. Forever."

Yes, of course. This wasn't insanity, it was reality. There was a reason I only remembered Dr Mellick's murder. That was the only one I'd committed. I'd brought him here for my army to take care of, but he was mine. I couldn't let them have the jewel in the crown.

"Is this real?" The question was to myself but the skins muttered with their gravelly voices.

"We are real. You are real. We are your army."

It still didn't seem to be true, but how could it not? I'd witnessed these things commit murder, taking their victims to be one of their own like a horde of leathery zombies. The pills had made me question everything, but I was free from those now.

"Why did you attack me here?" I snarled at them. "You call me your leader, yet you tried to kill me."

"It was a test, Master," said the congregation. "You had instructed us to attempt to destroy you. You said it would convince yourself that we were real and not just a symptom of your illness."

They spoke the truth. I remembered now. I'd been questioning this whole operation, but being a victim of their carnivorous rage had cemented the reality. They were never Dr Mellick's victims, they were mine. They were here to serve, they always had been. A plot to frame a man I knew to be my father had been my way of disguising the bloodlust from myself.

"Yes, and you served me well, soldiers."

Now I was ready to accept it all. It was me who had called the surgery, claiming I was Dr Mellick, complaining of a sickness bug that would keep me at home for a few days. Jill hadn't suspected a thing, she was far too concerned for the doctor's wellbeing to force an issue with me. Little did she know the real Dr Mellick would never be returning to work.

It was me who broke into my own house. I knew I'd return there later and panic that it was actually Dr Mellick who had been there.

The notebook in Dr Mellick's office? Of course it was me who'd been making notes in there. I even wrote my own name, safe in the knowledge I would react exactly as I had done. Suspecting Dr Mellick of killing me was all the motivation I needed to continue with my plan.

The lengths I went to to test myself. But they were necessary, and had worked perfectly. Convincing myself that I was imagining this whole thing had made this realisation all the more sweet. I tipped my metaphorical hat to my former self.

My army parted like a Biblical sea as I strode towards the open door.

"Kill them. Kill them all," I shouted. "Have them join us." The skins roared. Battle was upon us.

The corridor was equally infested with them. I sauntered past the ranks of soldiers like a king. I headed to the stairs. I needed to see this, every single kill would be a celebration of my gift.

"Stop. Police. Holy shit, what the *fuck*..." came a cry that reverberated from down the stairs.

Gunfire erupted.

"What the fuck are those things," howled another voice. The scream that followed was cut short in a split-second.

The skins growled like angry predators and fluttered past me to aid their brothers and sisters in the ensuing battle. I smiled.

Oh, how the feeble officers screamed. How they'd *all* scream. The skins flowed down the stairs like rats, ready to kill for me again.

The hospital was filling with skins and cops alike. More

gun shots. More screaming. More pleas for mercy. But my skins could never comprehend such kind sentiments. The sounds that bounced violently between the dilapidated walls were a symphony of despair.

The cops would keep on coming, backup for the backup. They would all be killed until no more were left to fight.

It would be over soon, I would be free to continue my work. Dr Mellick was dead and now I could follow what had always been my ultimate goal.

I wouldn't stop here. I'd replaced the pills with another drug, the high of suffering. Yes, my army of skin would soon be much stronger than I'd ever imagined. There would be no halting it. The numbers would increase exponentially. Before long the whole world would be part of my army.

I really *was* a King.

MORGAN K TANNER

Morgan K Tanner is a writer, drummer, and golfist currently residing in the English countryside. The idyllic surroundings make it an ideal place to write, drum, and hide the bodies. The busy sound of the typewriter is perfect to drown out the hum of the antiquated torture equipment. His works of fiction and threats have appeared in the mailboxes of many a celebrity, who then sells their story to the tabloids, claiming that they are being 'terrorized.'

You can praise or indeed abuse him by visiting www.morganktanner.com or find him on Twitter @morgantanner666.